Blood Mountain

By

Jacey K Dew

Chapter 1

"Hey Hunny. I was just calling to let you know I landed safely. I'm in the car, and on my way. I'll be hitting the mountains right away, so reception's going to be in and out. I'll call you after I get there. I miss you already. Love you forever and always. Hope you have great night. Bye." I leave my message feeling a bit awkward, and then end the call through the large red icon I know is there without looking.

Taking my eyes off the road for a second, I place the phone back on my dashboard and then put my eyes back on the road. Not much of the similar trees and rocks are missed for the few seconds it took, yet much of the road has passed with the excessive speed the car is travelling. Thinking back, I should have slowed down.

Pressing the mute button on the steering wheel brings back my music in a gradual evolution from quiet to booming.

A deep breath takes in the fresh mountain air. It's been five years since I have been anywhere near mountains. It would've been longer if I really had any say in the matter.

No, that's a lie.

I could have ignored my sister's plea to come home. I could have ignored that my mom was told that she had six months to live. I could not have requested to work from 'home' while I tend to things. I could have stayed with my fiancé. I could have told my sister that there is no way possible I could go home for six months. I could have ignored everything until mom's funeral.

In fact, I probably would have done all of that, if I didn't have such a caring fiancé back at home. She insisted that I do this. She said it would be good for me, and good for my family. And, she may be right.

I wouldn't be so reluctant to go home if home wasn't a small town in the crux of mountains. The nearest real anything is at least a couple hours away. There is no such thing as a big chain anything in this town.

Sure, they have a doctor and medical center, but you're screwed if you can't last a two hour trip to the hospital. That's even if you can actually drive on the roads leading out of town. Most winters there is some sort of snow pile up that makes the town inaccessible by regular vehicles.

Kara Walker

Why am I going back again?

Oh yes, I love my family. They are amazing people. I am thoroughly convinced that I had the perfect family growing up. My dad made the money, but was always home by supper and spent the evening spending time with us. My mom stayed at home, did everything, and loved us all to pieces. And my twin sister, whom I always got along with, was an amazing role model. I'm excited that I will finally be able to meet my two year old niece.

Most of that isn't true, or rather has only the barest hints of truth.

I straddle the faded line on the narrow mountain road. The edge of the road has always scared me. A fear of driving off the side of the mountain instilled in me when a classmate and her family swerved on the ice and shot off the side; the rails doing nothing to stop their descent. None of them survived the fall and subsequent crash. Pictures of the mangled car were plastered everywhere.

There is no one on this road. I haven't passed anyone since I got onto the road leading up the mountain paths. Not many people come out this far off the main road. There isn't any reason to unless you live in, or are visiting my town, or if you decide to take an extremely long detour to the next city; one in which you get to town and realize there is no way through so you back track to the 'Y' in the road.

When I round the mountain I can see the town's lights through the leafless trees. It will still be about ten minutes until I make it down there. I slow my speed to get down the switch back road. You never know what is around any of these corners. Growing up we were always hearing about what latest animal was on the road; goats, bears, coyotes, and moose mostly. Sometimes that went along with a totaled vehicle, and sometimes people had passed away.

The town is picturesque from afar. Nestled in the crux of the surrounding mountains is a two hundred building town; two thirds residential and one third businesses. The businesses sit at the start of the town; the lowest belly of the break in the mountains. The houses gradually go up the slightly inclined edges. One main road runs through the center of it all.

I swear the town hasn't changed at all since I left. Not one thing. The Drugs sign is still off kilter. All the buildings need a fresh coat of paint. I'm pretty sure drunken Will's vehicle has been parked at the bar since I left.

Two blocks in and take a right. The Café looks exactly like it did when I left. The only thing to change in the log building, I'm sure over the last five years, is that my sister now works here.

Kara Walker

I park in the small parking lot next to the Café. My car looks out of place between old trucks, and SUV's. There's rust, and caked mud on all of them, while my car is a new and shiny rental.

The doors are smoothed on the wooden handles where everyone always touches. The rest of the door looks worn and rough.

The moment I get through the door, I smell the amazing mishmash scent of all the home made dishes the owner makes from scratch every day. My stomach growls in anticipation of the addicting chicken fingers and milk shakes.

The inside looks the same as always; country home style chic. Each table is all ready for customers; white table clothes, cutlery set on either side of where your plate would go, and menu in place of the plate. There are fake flowers set out in vases everywhere. Children's drawings are hung on the walls.

There isn't anyone around out here, but I can hear voices in the back. I didn't make much noise when I came in, so I don't think they heard me. I certainly make out the sound of my sister's voice, and that of Mrs. Whitter.

I feel brave enough to hop behind the counter, but not brave enough to go through the doors into the back. There is a serving counter that has a window to the kitchen. They have a bell they normally use to tell the waiters and waitresses that an order is ready.

I ring the bell. In the most dramatic way I can muster I say, "Can I get some service here? I'm starving and I've been waiting here forever."

Just as I can recognize her voice, I can also recognize her excited scream. The door to my right swings open hard, Sara comes running out, and tackle hugs me. She almost knocks me off balance and we stumble to stay upright. The counter behind knocks into my back, and we finally stop moving. I wince from digging edge.

She pushes herself away from me to look at me, and then pulls me into another hug. The first thing I notice about her is how thin she's gotten. Worry lines and purple circles under her eyes speak to her stress and exhaustion. We used to mirror each other, but now she appears older; not in a good way.

Sara still looks pretty much the same otherwise, though a tiny bit more grown up. Her brown hair is tied up in a ponytail, but I can tell she's grown out her hair. When it's down I would bet it goes to, at least, three quarters down her back. Her naturally tan skin is the lightest it gets naturally, so I can assume she didn't get much sun this summer.

"Let her breathe. You get her to yourself for the next few months. Besides I want a hug too." Mrs. Whitter lightly pulls Sara away from me, just to take her place. She pulls slightly away from me to place her wrinkled hand on my cheek. "I am so happy you decided to come. I only wish you would stay longer. Now get out from behind my counter or I'll ban you." When she's done admonishing me, she turns me around and lightly pushes me towards the counter exit. I can't help but to giggle and blush lightly from getting in trouble. She makes me feel like a teenager again.

She lifts the counter top up for me and lets me pass through. I take a seat at the counter and pull up a menu from a stack. The menu hasn't changed at all.

"She'll have a strawberry milkshake and chicken fingers and fries." Sara orders for me. The menu is wrenched from my hands and placed back where I had taken it. She pulls out a wet cloth from under the counter and wipes off my invisible fingerprints.

"Of course she will. With my honey mustard sauce too." Mrs. Whitter agrees with Sara, and then goes into the kitchen. Sara follows right after her. Shortly after, I can hear the blender going. Sara comes out with a tall glass full of strawberry milkshake and the extra in the silver mixing cup. I grab two straws from the counter. When she puts both cups in front of me I pour a bit from the glass back into the tin one. I stick a straw in both and shove the tin cup back at her.

"Drink."

She looks too long and too hard about it before she grabs the drink from me. The look of sheer pleasure on her face, before guilt bleeds into her eyes makes me wonder how long it's been since she's indulged on something so sugary.

Oh, I should text Lainey before I forget again. I pull out my phone, and go into the messaging icon. She's the last contact I texted so it pulls up my conversation with her automatically. I start typing.

Hey, I'm here safe and sound. I'm having supper with my sister. I'll call you later tonight. Love you. Miss you already. XOXO - Kara

I press the send button. The phone thinks and thinks. Holding it up and waving it I wait until the message shows that it actually sent before turning off the phone screen, and putting it in my pocket.

I take a few gulps of my thick shake. The straw gets blocked. I pull my straw out of the liquid, and eat the strawberry chunk blocking the bottom of the straw.

"So when do I get to meet my niece?" I ask a bit awkwardly. I didn't think a conversation would be hard to make with my sister. Now that I think about it, our phone conversations have been becoming a less frequent thing over the last few years. We used to talk almost every day, and the days I wasn't talking with her, I was talking with mom. Slowly, that's become a conversation with either mom or Sara maybe every six months; once on their birthdays, and maybe one or two other times through the year.

Whose fault is that? Mine, hers, or moms? All of ours?

"She's at mom's house. She's babysitting while I'm at work. You can head over there when you're done supper. I'm off at ten, so I'll head over then." Sara goes on. "You still remember how to get there?"

"Of course. Even if I didn't, this place really isn't that big. Go down Main Street, up the mountain to the houses, down to the road after the neon yellow house, turn right, and down to the last house on the left." I answer.

"What if the Gerald's painted their house?" Her question stops me for a minute.

"Then I'd be screwed." I laugh. I really would be. I mean I'd eventually be able to find it, but not without going down a few wrong roads. I really hope that she's joking about them painting their house. "They didn't paint their house did they?"

She smiles her crazy smile. "No, but if they ever did I'd bet it would be some other god awful colour. You'd be fine." We both laugh at that. Their house looks like they had taken a yellow highlighter to it. They'd probably pick a different highlighter if they ever painted their house again.

"How was your flight?" Mrs. Whitter asks as she comes out from the back. She comes around to my side of the counter and puts the plate down in front of me. My mouth waters from the smell of my food. Nostalgia wafts into my head through my nose.

I try to think about what to tell them exactly. There was a guy next to me that kept getting up to use the bathroom. There was a couple that had a crying baby on the flight. "It was okay. There was a little bit of turbulence, but not too bad. I've never really liked flying, but you can't argue with the time saved. It would take a day to drive what you can fly in a few hours."

"So tell me everything. Assume your sister and your mom have told me nothing. I want to know what you've been up to since you left us." Mrs. Whitter probably knows everything that I've told either my mom or Sara. It's a small town, and everyone talks. No one ever leaves; except me. I'm sure that I've come up in topic more than once since I left. Whether with rumours or the truth, people would have talked about me.

However, I figure that I will indulge her; I'll have to do the same with everyone in this town. "Umm, well I had a small apartment with a roommate. He was really nice. I had a job at McDonald's for a couple of years while I went to school for business and marketing. Got picked up by a marketing company and now I work with them figuring out new promos, and setting up the promotions for our clients. I met my fiancé in one of my classes. I live with her now. Life's going good. What about here? I'm sure there are tonnes of small town gossip I've missed out on."

I let Sara and Mrs. Whitter talk for the next hour. I eat my delicious chicken fingers and fries, and finish the shake. Other than a couple words here and there I don't say much. I just listen to the gossip from the last five years. Who knew there could be so much? It's mostly who got together with whom, who got married, who hooked up, and who cheated on whom.

When I start yawning Mrs. Whitter stops her gossip chatter. "Why don't you two girls go home? It's a slow night, and I bet you want to be there when Kara meets Caitlyn." Mrs. Whitter picks up the dirty dishes in front of us. "This one's on me. Go get your coat, and go on home."

"You sure you don't need me to stay?" Sara asks, though I know she's just trying to be nice.

In her head she's already out the door.

I know there isn't much use in arguing with Mrs. Whitter on this, so I say, "thank you, you didn't have to do that," while I get up from my seat.

"You're welcome Kare. Sara, I'm not going to say it again. I'm going to put these in the sink and you better not be here when I get back out here." She opens the door using her elbow, and disappears into the kitchen.

Sara reaches for the coat rack behind the counter. She grabs a white winter coat. "Thank you, have a great night!" I echo these same words right after Sara.

We both run out of the café as fast as we can. I feel giddy, like we just got out of school early. Now were going to run home to mom and play.

It's ridiculous how many memories and old feelings come up just by spending a couple hours back in my home town. I can thank Lainey for this later. If it wasn't for her I wouldn't be here right now; feeling all nostalgic about the good old days.

"So, which one's yours?" I ask her. Wrapping my arms in a self hug to keep some of my warmth. I forgot how much colder the evenings can be.

"Don't have one. No license either. I walk

everywhere. You forget it only takes a half hour to walk from one end of town to the other. I don't need my own vehicle." Sara explains. I remember, but that still doesn't mean that she shouldn't have her license, or her own vehicle. What if something happens? She gets hurt, or mom does, or Caitlyn? Is she going to try to get a hold of someone, and wait for them to arrive? I don't say anything to her back but I nod.

Her response would probably be to take mom's car and drive illegally. No one would stop her here; not without good reason. Not that she'd get in trouble if she was driving for an emergency either.

We load up into my car. I wrap my seatbelt around myself and turn on the car. I wait for her to put on her seatbelt but she doesn't. Small town mentality; I'm not going far so I won't wear a seatbelt. I don't know whether to say something or not. I mean, really it's up to her. She's only putting herself at risk for greater injury if we get into an accident. Unless, she were to fly out of her seat towards me. And, I'd probably get blamed because I didn't make her wear one. Her child would be without her mom.

I should say something. "Seat belt."

She looks at me like I've grown another head. "I don't wear them. I don't like how they feel. Besides, were not going far."

"I'd prefer you'd wear one when I'm driving you around." She does as I ask and puts it on, but she does so begrudgingly. I'd rather she get upset with me than injured because she doesn't wear one.

It's a silent ride after that. She wants to be mad, fine. She'll stop once we get there.

I go up the hill to the residential part of town. Driving straight I almost wonder if her joke was real; that the bright yellow house has been painted over. I get a sinking feeling that I've gone too far. I don't remember the turn being this far.

Then, I see it. I'm sure the yellow has actually intensified while I've been gone. I turn right and go down to the end. The two story house stands tall in a one story neighbourhood. We've got the tallest house in the town, but it's not the biggest. No living space in the basement it's just a small cellar only accessible from the outside. The main floor has the kitchen, bathroom, and living room. The upstairs is divided into two halves; my parent's room on the one side and the room Sara and I shared growing up.

I pull into the driveway and roll to a stop. Before I even have the vehicle turned off Sara is unclasping her seatbelt and opening her door. I put in the emergency break, and turn off the car. I unbuckle myself and follow her to the door.

Kara Walker

She walks right in.

I guess mom still doesn't lock the doors.

"Caitlyn, mom, I'm here and I brought someone with me." Sara yells loud enough they should be able to hear her throughout the whole house.

Closing the door behind me, I take off my boots, and tuck them beside a very small set of Velcro runners. A very small person appears at the top of the stairs. Instantly, I'm afraid she's going to fall down them. Whether she can use them or not, she is way too excited and I'm sure she's just going to leap down.

And, she does. She just about gives me a heart attack, but Sara got halfway up the stairs while my attention was on Caitlyn. Sara catches the little girl and they have a laugh about it. I resist the urge to tell both of them that isn't safe at all. Sara could miss catching Caitlyn, or Caitlyn could send Sara off balance.

I just smile, as Sara brings Caitlyn to me. "Auntie Mommy." The little girl says before she reaches out both of her arms for me to take her. Apparently, Sara or mom have talked about me and shown her pictures enough times that she knows exactly who I am. Not that it wouldn't be hard to just say I look exactly like Sara. My eyes collect more moisture briefly from how touched this makes me feel.

"Hi Caitlyn. Wow you're so big." I add the 'and heavy' in my mind as I settle her down on my hip. I've never done this before, not with anyone quite so big. Sure I've held an infant before, but he was a few months old and about a quarter of her size. I give her a bit of a squeeze as a hug.

I look her over trying to do a quick comparison of which parent she looks like. I haven't seen Cody in a few years but I'm going to say she got pretty much everything from him; blue eyes, red hair, and pointed features. The mixture of his and her skin colour have created a light spring tan natural colouring; lighter than hers and darker than his.

"Kare." A cold harsh voice calls my nickname. Mom stands at the top of the stairs, but she doesn't look like the mom I remember. She looks sick. She's lost a lot of weight; her skin is really pale and wrinkled. She has dark circles all around her eyes. Mom looks like she's aged twenty years over the last five.

It appears to have been a theme with the women in this house hold; a physical symptom of the stress they've undergone.

Unlatching the girl from my hip, I set her down on the floor. I walk upstairs to my mom and hug her. She's slightly sticky with sweat. "You should be resting. What were you doing?"

"Oh hush, I was setting up the guest room for you. You should be thanking me." She waves her hand in front of her to bat away my words of gratitude. Mom turns around and walks into my room. What used to be half my room; with two beds, two dressers, drawings and pictures, posters, and trinkets. Following her inside I find one double bed, a crib, and one dresser.

She changed my room. More likely, Sara had changed our room, but I feel like blaming mom for this one. I mean I've been gone for five years. I took a lot of my stuff with me when we left. But, still it kind of hurts that she would just completely change everything.

"You're going to share with Caitlyn. She's only here half the time, so every other week you'll have the room to yourself." Mom says.

"I thought you had full custody." Erupts from my mouth while I search for answers in Sara's eyes.

She shakes her head, and heart break waters her eyes. "It's stupid. Cody asked for custody of her and just because he asked the judge awarded him half custody."

I don't really know how much I should say in front of Caitlyn. I don't know how much language she knows, nor what she might pick up and repeat back to Cody.

"So what? None of the past matters. He asked nicely and got half custody." I sum up my understanding of exactly what she had just said, rage tightening my voice.

"Pretty much. Judge said that none of my proof mattered because what happened was between me and him. Because he's never done anything to Caitlyn specifically, he can have access to her and half custody. One week I have her and one week he has her; repeat. Because I didn't report things that I should have to the sheriff, at the time they happened."

"That's dumb." Little ears make me substitute what I actually wish to say; a long string of swears.

"Family court is messed up. And now he's got Darla pregnant." My eyes widen in surprise at the revelation. "Ya, they are eight months along and have been together for nine months. She's living with him, and going to be a stay at home mom. And, because of that, he's going after full custody. He's petitioning the court for full custody because he says I'm an unfit mother." Sara seethes at the end.

"Are you kidding me? That's disgusting." How can he accuse her of being an unfit mother? It makes no sense. He's the unfit parent. He shouldn't even be allowed near Caitlyn, and yet the system already allows him to; orders her to let him.

Sara's appearance makes sense now. The stress of everything piled on her must be exhausting.

She takes care of mom. She has a toddler. She constantly has to deal with her rapist wife beater ex-husband. She has to say goodbye to her little girl for a week every other week. She says goodbye never knowing if that's the last time she's going to see her. Not knowing what is happening to her.

My heart breaks for Sara. I wish there was more I did. I shouldn't have stayed away this long.

A wet throaty cough fills the house. Sara immediately runs out to locate mom; who disappeared in our conversation. This attack is likely from her effort to prep my room. I give the coughing a minute to die down. When they do, I decide to bring my bags inside and unpack. Sara can handle mom for the moment. I'll watch Caitlyn.

"Do you want to come help me bring in my things?" I ask the little girl.

She throws up her arms. "Upidy," she says. My niece is so adorable. A simple smile melts my heart.

I pick her up and drag her downstairs with me.

"Wait here. I will go grab my bags and bring them inside."

Her response is to whine, and grab her shoes. I guess she's coming outside with me.

Full gear is needed for her to venture outside. Suited in shoes and her jacket she's properly dressed to go outside.

I slip on my boots, and open the door. We collect my bags and quickly return to our room.

She wastes no time to open my bags and go through them. Caitlyn is in her heyday going through all my things. Nothing is put away by the time Sara comes back.

"Are you having fun?" She asks.

"It's fun going through other people's things." I explain in place of Caitlyn; who doesn't have the words yet to explain it herself.

"Of course."

"Snoopy; just like her mom." I poke fun at her.

"Just like her auntie." Sara takes her own jab back at me.

I'm surprised at how quickly things have returned to normal. How fast we have been able to step into our roles despite the time that has passed.

Chapter 2

The familiar smell of cigarettes pierces my nose. I blow out a breath through my nostrils to clear them and the disgusting smell. I put the mug back and grab another. This one passes the sniff test.

I should buy new mugs for this place. There is only one handful which is safe to use now. Mom's *secret* habit of smoking and stashing the butts in mugs all over the house has consequently destroyed most of the mugs. The others still use them though. They are nose blind to the stench.

One half a fleeting thought to just use Caitlyn's colourful plastic cups passes because she goes through them fast enough without my using them too.

I fill the cup up with piping hot milk, and two tablespoons of the hot chocolate mix. Stirring the mixture together, until all the clumps dissolve to be one with the liquid.

A cry fills the room from the baby monitor placed on the table.

I sigh. The most productive part of my work day has been the last hour and a half she's been asleep. I set down the hot chocolate and rush upstairs to collect her. Mom is asleep too, and I'd hate for her to wake up. This morning was a disaster of passive aggressive remarks and side eyed glares.

Opening the door quietens the cries slightly as she realizes she'll be freed in just a moment. "Shhh. It's okay. I'm here."

I pull her out of the crib and wrap her in a big hug. Her cries turn to whimpers. Once I step foot out of the room she stops her noises entirely.

She grasps tightly onto my neck as I descend. Caitlyn launches herself backwards. My heart stops as I imagine her falling, but my arm stops her. She dangles there until my other hand catches up to pull her upright.

"Don't do that." I gasp out. She just laughs. "You scared me." The tiny toddler laughs some more as if it was some sort of hilarious joke. I huff and smile. She's crazy; just like my sister.

She's bound to be hungry. She's been eating right after her afternoon nap as soon as she's been waking up. Supper is about two hours later, and a second supper when Sara comes home.

Tomorrow our little schedule will change with Sara's day off. I'm excited for it.

After I sit her on the couch and turn on the TV to whatever child show is playing, I go into the kitchen to peruse the pantry and fridge for a little snack.

I cut up an apple and place it on a plastic plate. Mom always makes her sit at the table to eat, but I just put the plate beside her on the couch. I don't see any issue with a little food on the couch. Mom is asleep, and dad took off long ago.

No one should get in trouble.

"No no apple." Caitlyn pushes the plate away. My quick reflexes aren't fast enough to stop the plate from bouncing off the floor, and the apples spilling around everywhere.

I sigh. Those apples are useless now. The carpet hair, and everything collected within them will have contaminated the apple slices. I'm not feeding Caitlyn those apples, even if I were to wash them off. I don't know how good her immune system is, but I do know I wouldn't eat them

"What do you want for a snack? Do you know what you want to eat?" I ask her a little frustrated.

To my surprise she slides herself off the couch. I reach over to steady her and catch her if she falls, but she manages perfectly on her own.

The tiny toddler takes off for the kitchen on sure and steady feet. Torn between cleaning the mess and running after Caitlyn I choose the later. She can't be unsupervised at this age and the apples can always be cleaned up a little later.

She stands at the fridge waiting for me with her hands up reaching for the door handles. She knows what they are and how to get into the fridge, but I don't think she has the strength yet to pull the doors open.

I help her out. She ducks so the doors don't hit her head. With the French doors wide open a person can see everything in the upper portion.

She points with vigour towards something high above her. "This." Caitlyn says. "This."

"What do you want?" I ask her to clarify. Maybe she doesn't have the words for it yet; maybe she does and isn't using it.

I pick her up so she can show me what she wants. Her feet fit nicely on the freezer door. She stands there using me for balance, but she doesn't necessarily need it. She grabs the cheese from the top shelf.

I put her on the ground and take the cheese from her. She shuts the doors by herself.

She impresses me with how much she does and knows. I always expect her to be more like a baby, but then she does little responsible acts without even being asked.

I shake my head to shake myself out of the moment. She wants cheese, so I cut it up for her. I place it on a plastic plate for her and hand it over.

She takes her plate to the table and places it on top. The little girl pulls out her own seat and climbs to a seated position. Happily she munches on her snack.

With her momentary preoccupation I can return to work. My forgotten hot chocolate sits on the counter. I grab it and take a drink. It's no longer hot, but it's a good warm for a drink of its kind.

Sitting at the opposite end of the table, I sip my liquid chocolate and peruse my work email.

It doesn't take long for her to finish her little snack. She pushes off her chair and runs off back to the apple slices I had forgotten about.

I rush over to grab the slice before a slice goes into her mouth. "Gross. Yucky. Don't put that in your mouth."

"What is she doing with apples in the living room?" The hard tone comes straight out of my mother's mouth. "You know better than that."

"Sorry." I say reflexively.

We've not said much to each other since I

returned, and I don't imagine that will change. For the rest of her life, I will be blessed with nothing more than passive aggressive remarks, negatively turned phrases, and courtesy phrases. She will never forgive me as she is the most stubborn woman I have ever met, and I went against her wishes in so many ways.

"You're lucky your father isn't here to see that." Her disapproving stare turns my gaze to the floor.

My answer is silence.

There is no arguing with my mother.

The front door opens. I stand up in a flash ready to run or defend myself from the intruder before I remember where I am. Big crime rarely happens here. No one ever locks their doors. There isn't a need to lock them like there is back home.

"Why isn't she ready to go?" Cody's voice booms after he walks in view of the living room.

"Hi Cody. I didn't know she was supposed to go with you today." I rush the words out honestly.

"That's bullshit. You know our schedule. You're just trying to rob me of my time with Caitlyn." His voice thunders.

"You done? I'm Kara." The hostility instantly

relaxes at the reveal of my true identity.

"Hi Kara. Where's your mom? Where's Sara?" I try not to be offended at his lack of a welcome back but we were never really that close.

"Sara's at work. Mom-"

"Right here. Hello Cody. She's almost ready to go. Kare, go get Caitlyn's bag from her bedroom." Mom walks out from the kitchen down the hall. She gives him a big hug.

I double take Cody while I walk by him. He looks the same as he did in high school as the jock dating my sister. He is a tank of a man; impossibly tall and large. A bit of a gut has protruded from his belly as an ode to his beer obsession.

I listen to their conversation as I bound up the stairs. Snoopy as ever, I listen to their interaction and the undertones.

"I'm sorry I'm late today. I should be on time next round. Darla had a scan. You know how that doctor stuff always takes so long." Cody fills the silence.

I reach our room and easily spot the away bag. Grabbing it then taking it back down stairs. I hand it to Cody.

"Yes, you'd think they don't know you have

other places to be. God forbid you're late one minute, but they have no problem wasting your whole day." She commiserates with him.

I smile at their exchange. At lease they are amicable. I doubt the hand off would go so well if Sara were here. Cody's mistaken identity earlier proves his hostility toward my sister.

Now he's laughing and cheerful.

One body is missing, that of the little toddler who's to join her father.

"I'll go find Caitlyn." I say but I doubt they hear it.

Half way into the living room mom calls after me. "Check the pantry. She always hides in there."

"Okay." My first stop is the pantry in the kitchen. There is no need to go further when I spot the little girl with her hands over her eyes.

"Hey sweetie, time to go with your dad." I reach out for her.

She backs away as far as she can and swats my away. "No, no, no, no, no, no, no, no, no. No, daddy no. No go. No go."

Her words confuse me for just a moment. Then, they break my heart. Caitlyn doesn't want to leave. She doesn't want to go with her dad.

Considering the circumstances I'm leaning towards the likely hood that Caitlyn doesn't want to visit her dad as much as Sara doesn't want her to be with him. Why isn't that taken into consideration when they do custody battles?

Then again, many a loving parent has this same battle with their child; do they not? A toddler picks favourites and will throw a temper tantrum when the favourite tries to pass off to the other one for something as small as a bathroom break.

"Just grab her and bring her here." Mom yells irritated from the entry way.

Though it seems harsh I pull her up into an embrace. Her small body puts up a resistance unlike any other I've encountered. Her earlier thrust is now amplified with each twist. My only thought is to hug her to me so I don't drop her.

I barely notice the big arms until they are almost around Caitlyn's waist. "Let her go. I've got her."

I do as he says. He wrangles to churning body into a hug of his own. Caitlyn's scream amplifies when she realizes what is happening. Her little face is red and real tears are on her cheeks. She reaches out for me. I can't help but to reach out for her.

I can't watch her leave. My face already burns

with the need to cry. It doesn't take them much longer to say their goodbyes and leave the house. Her screaming doesn't stop until she's too far to hear; I fear they will continue long after that.

When the door closes I watch my mom sets herself in her chair. She grabs her laptop, turns on the TV and lights up a smoke. I roll my eyes in disgust. Not one more word is said.

I grab my laptop and move my work upstairs.

Not one more word is said until Sara comes knocking at the door. "I brought supper. Mom said you were being a shut in up here."

"Just as much company up here as there would have been down there." I offer.

"Touché." Behind the door frame she pulls out a take away dinner from the diner. "Chicken fingers and fries." Sara answers the unasked question. I open the container placed in front of me and grab one to shovel into my mouth. My stomach signals it's hunger. "How's work going?" She asks in true waiter fashion; to wait until food has been shoved into the mouth to ask a question.

I raise my eyebrow and just watch her until I finish the piece in my mouth. She smiles real big when she realizes what she did. "Good. I was able to catch up today. I didn't get much work done in the morning, but I expected that because I was mostly playing with Caitlyn. I got some work done while she napped, then she got up for a snack. And then, Cody got her. I was able to catch up on everything the last few hours."

Sara frowns instantly. "Hours? When did Cody pick her up?"

Immediately, I know something is wrong. "He picked her up after her nap around two. Said he was late picking her up. I assumed he was supposed to grab her up in the morning." I spill all the information I can as I see her increasingly angered snarl.

"He's supposed to pick her up at six pm; no earlier. It is part of our agreement."

"It sounded like a pretty regular thing between mom and him." I add in part to get mom in trouble and in part because it's a truth that she needs to be aware of.

Her face practically turns red. She throws herself up off the bed. Sara stomps to the door. "Mom! MOM!"

"In the living room." Her muffled voice calls.

Sara stampedes down the stairs. Aware of the fight about to break out I rush to follow her. Someone might need to referee this so the yelling match doesn't get out of hand. Or, so I can better help Sara when mom says all the nasty things she is bound to say.

"Mom, did you let Cody pick Caitlyn up early?"

I lean against the wall just at the edge of the room. I'll interfere if it goes too far.

"It was only a few hours." Mom demeans with her tone and demeanour.

"How long have you been letting him pick her up early?" Sara's voice squeaks in the beginning; something which only happens when she is truly angry.

"It's not like you were home sweety. I hardly see why letting him pick her up early is a problem when you're not even spending the time with her." Mom redirects the question. She won't answer because it's likely be going on for a while. Her health hasn't been the best for the last few months so I wouldn't doubt that it began then. I wouldn't doubt if it's happened before that due to her laziness.

"Because I have to work, and that is not the point! It's the principal. He gets one week with her and I get one week with her. It's not one week minus a few hours because I have to work to support my mother." This argument feels like its hit the turning point, and has me straightening from the electricity.

Mom finally acknowledges Sara with an

annoyed stare. "Well you always complain about him shoving her off to his parents, and why doesn't he just let you take her if she's going to spend the whole time not with him. It works both ways sweetheart." She patronizes Sara.

Sara practically growls. "That's because he sends her to his parents so he can get high and drink all he wants. He doesn't want to be a parent. He just takes her so he can continue to ruin my life and torture me!"

"It takes two to make a child. If you didn't want a kid with him you should have kept your legs shut. If you didn't want to be away from Caitlyn you should have stayed with him."

Sara slicks her hair back. "That wasn't an option. He would have ended up killing me."

Mom points her finger to Sara's face. "Stop being so dramatic, Sara. He's with another girl and they are working out just fine. Maybe if you weren't so hot headed you'd be one happy family."

"I'm not the only issue-"

Mom interrupts Sara. "I was there. You treated him like dirt. You were a spoiled brat and when he would stand up for himself you would scream at him."

"I defended myself. I was the one who needed to defend myself. You didn't see everything."

"Stop playing the victim because you screwed up your chance at a good life with a good man." It's rich to hear that coming from someone who screwed up her marriage. I can't believe mom is victim blaming her daughter.

"Do you need to see the scar again, mom? From where he *accidentally* stabbed me with a knife." This is a new revelation to me. My heart drops. No one told me Cody stabbed Sara.

How does this man not have a restraining order against him? How does he have half custody of Caitlyn? How is he not in jail?

She doesn't wait for a response, and lifts up her shirt. I try to see a scar, but there isn't anything on her back. The stab must have been to the front and didn't go all the way through.

Even in my rage for her, I manage to contain it to a dull glare just so I can support her in this altercation. I want so badly to throw something and I'm glad there isn't anything within arm's reach.

"He barely scratched you." Mom chides her.

"He threw a knife at me because I had put a knife in the sink instead of on the counter. He threw it at me because he touched it and *thought* he cut himself." Sara puts a lot of pressure on the word 'thought' to emphasize it.

"You should never put sharp knives in the

sink; that's dangerous. I'm sure he had told you many times not to do so, but you never listen." Mom reprimands.

"You're impossible!" Sara explodes.

"You're impossible." Mom echoes.

"Fuck you! I hate you!" Sara announces venomously. She doubles back to me.

When Sara runs by me, not one part of me wants to check on our mother and comfort her. There is nothing but distain for her. Not one part of that fight was anything like a loving mother should be having with their daughter.

All the pain she has caused is nothing she will ever be forgiven for; at least from my end.

I follow behind Sara and into our bedroom. She stands at the door, and the moment I clear the space I hear a distinct bang from the door slamming shut; it makes me jump.

It's her signature move, from when we were children, to let our parents know how upset she was. Usually, though, it just ended in more scolding.

"Did you want to sleep in here tonight?" I offer, more than ask because I know what her answer will be.

"Please."

We sit in silence on the bed for a moment. She snaps up one of my cold chicken fingers and starts gulping it down. I snatch one for myself because I know I won't get any if she continues on with her angered eating.

I eat my chicken finger waiting for the talk about to come. After a few revelations downstairs, I know she has a lot to talk about. We've gone beyond the pleasantries of the first few days in reacquainting one another and now the nitty gritty details are emerging from the deep pits they'd been thrown into.

"God." She breathes in deep. "I know. She says these things to hurt me, but part of me has thought the same things; you know. I stayed with him because I was pregnant. He was a jerk before; you know. I got pregnant and at first he seemed happy, then distant, and then half way through he got drunk and threatened to push me down the stairs so I would lose the baby. But I stayed because I thought he might stop using for me. I thought he might return to just being a jerk. Then I stayed because I had a newborn baby. He convinced me I was the problem because I had post partem depression. But, I found the courage to leave him when my maternity leave was up. He was forcing me to go back to work even though we had agreed I would be a stay at home mom. Once I was back at work I got a boost of confidence and stupidly thought he'd leave us alone. Women shouldn't have to stay with their abusers because they are worried about their babies. Men should lose all right to their children if they abuse their mom. It's that or courts award half custody and the moms have to worry if the bastard is going to take off and disappear, or hit her when he gets mad, or yell because he's high and drunk, or kill her in a fit. I even tried going back to him, but he had already gotten another girl pregnant. I wanted to be with a man that raped me, abused me and threatened to kill me, just so I wouldn't lose my baby half the time; at the barest minimum."

Her confessions have my gut wrenched. The pain she had gone through is ridiculous. I should have been there.

"You shouldn't have to do that. Can you do something, anything? Get the court to make him do a drug test." I try to come up with anything I can to help, but I would think she's tried everything by now.

"I tried. They don't do drug tests by request. I would basically have to catch him high while he's watching Caitlyn, and call the cops on him. Hope the cops book him for being high, and then I could maybe use it in court."

"That's a bit ridiculous. And, wouldn't work here because everyone basically just ignores the drug problem."

"Exactly." She chomps defeated into a fry. "I've spent about ten thousand dollars trying to fight him in court. I can't afford to keep this up."

One question burns on the tip of my tongue, and has since we were downstairs. "Why didn't you tell me all of this was happening?"

She looks away and refuses to look me in the eye. "You know, I mean, it sounds dumb. I ignored the warning signs. He always had a violent temper, but never towards me. He'd just freak out at the smallest thing. An egg yolk could break and he'd throw the frying pan. I wrote it off as that was just how he was; no problem. We'd have our fights now and then, but I never thought anything was wrong with it. Not like we had the best role models for relationships growing up. I thought that was normal. Then I got pregnant and things were good, until they weren't. I passed where I could get an abortion, that I was comfortable with anyway, so I felt stuck. I still thought we'd spend our lives together so I stayed and didn't tell anyone there was anything wrong. I thought maybe things would change once I had the baby. I thought I was the problem because of pregnancy hormones. But, I wasn't. It didn't get better. There were points I just wished he would overdose and die; still do. But, he hasn't so I have to deal with him. I will have to deal with him until she turns fourteen and can decide if she wants contact with him."

"Fourteen? That seems a little old."

Sara shrugs. "That's the law."

"But kids know. They know if they don't want to be around someone. They have minds of their own. Even at five years old a kid should have say in their own custody agreements. At five years old a kid can say 'I don't want to go with daddy because he's really mean. He yells at me and calls me names and I'm scared of him.' Shouldn't that be taken into consideration?"

"I know. It's stupid, but they think that a kid that age could be manipulated into saying something like that."

They may have a point. A mom could hate the dad and tell the kid to say lies to the judge just to gain full custody; just to spite the father. "I can see the point. But, I can think that it would at least prompt an investigation."

Just outside the door I hear mom hacking her lungs out. Sara gets up to help her. Even after the awful things said Sara still helps her.

She's better than I am.

I'd let her cough until she suffocated and died.

Chapter 3

A blast of heat and a small chime welcomes me into the small bank. Nothing has changed except for one picture hanging on the wall. The face of a familiar schoolmate hangs under his father.

It's unfortunate that he chose the life his father wanted for him despite his hatred for the financial world and his love for mechanics.

"I'll be right there." The younger familiar voice calls out from the office.

"Hey Alex, it's Kara." I announce. Better to do it before he sees me.

Something falls against the floor in a thud. Furniture scraps against the floor as a grunt of pain follows quickly after. A slightly older Alex emerges from the room. His hair, which used to trail half way down his back is now cut in a buzz cut. It's a shame, really. He always had prettier, luscious, and more well taken care of locks than any woman I've ever known. "Kara? What are you doing back in town?"

"Mom is sick." I trail off because I don't know how much everyone knows. No one's really brought it up, but it is a small nosy town.

He nods. "Yes, of course. I'm glad you were able to make it to visit her."

"Yes, it's good." My voice is unsure and trails off a little. "Helps Sara out a lot," I add as a second thought.

"That's good. Is there something I could do for you, or were you just visiting?" He cuts to the chase after little small talk.

"Is your dad here?" I ask. Alex's expression drops a little in disappointment.

"No, he's got the morning shift." His words bring hope to the reason I am here. His father was always a stickler for rules.

I pull out the mortgage slip from my purse. "I need to talk about this."

The sheet of paper is passed to the man, and he quickly looks it over. Alex immediately recognizes what it is. "I can't talk about details with you because you're not on the mortgage."

"Did I mention I was Sara acting like Kara to see if I could fool you into disclosing the information? You passed." The words are right, but the tone conveys the falsity of them. He'd be a fool to not understand.

His smile widens and he holds out his hand to point at the comfortable black leather chair at the teller's dark stained wooden desk. "In that case, take a seat."

"Thank you." I sit down at the customer side of the desk while he goes around to sit on his designated side. He turns on the screen of the computer with a swipe of the mouse. Fingers type furiously as he opens up the required account information. "Is that really the amount left on the mortgage?"

"Yes." Alex says simply as he barely glances at the screen.

"How?" I ask incredulous of his answer.

He reads the computer screen before he responds. "Your mom and Sara signed for a mortgage to be taken out. Dad had handled it; mostly." Most of his attention is on reviewing what happened so his speech goes in and out. If his dad handled the transaction he might not know everything he would need to.

That doesn't really tell me anything. I pry further. "Why? The house should have been paid off or close to it."

"It was almost done. Your mom sold the house to Sara, but Sara needed a cosigner so we put your mom on there too. Essentially we worked it in the system so that the house received a second mortgage and we added Sara's name and removed your father's name."

The words from his mouth don't sound right; it can't be legal to do what he's detailing. More and more this situation is crawling under my skin. Unlawful small town antics have their name written all over this. "So, Sara owns the house?"

"Yes and your mom."

"Right." I try to obtain clarification by detailing my understanding. "So, Sara was buying the house but didn't qualify. Then, mom took out a second mortgage and you slapped Sara's name on it in place of dad's name. So mom has all that money, and Sara is paying you for the mortgage. When mom dies then the house would go to Sara and not our father."

"Essentially, but the payments are coming from your mom's account right now. She said that Sara would pay her the money, and they have it worked out."

I wipe my forehead and leave my hand with my fingers pressed against the end of my eyebrow. "That doesn't make sense. Why would mom sell the house to Sara to have the money come out of her account, when the names could have been switched for what was left, and Sara and mom work out their own payments between each other?" The long worded, over complicated question is asked more to me than him.

"Your mom wanted the house to go to Sara and not your father, since they are still married. She said that she never plans on actually divorcing your father so when the day comes that she does die that she doesn't want to leave the chance that he'll try to claim the house." He says nothing more than what I could have speculated. It doesn't do much to answer my question.

I interrupt more of his response in my frustration. "So a second mortgage for two hundred grand made more sense than putting it in a will, or adding Sara to the existing mortgage and erasing our father's name, or selling the house for whatever was left of the existing mortgage?"

"It was the way your mother requested-" He trails off. Alex stares at the screen trying to gain any more information he would need to explain all of this. "It doesn't make sense to me either, but the customer's requests don't always make sense."

"Does Sara know about this?"

He nods his head. "Yes, she delivered the signed papers herself. I was there for that."

That means nothing to me. Mom could've asked a rushed Sara to sign papers and deliver to the bank before work. Sara would trust mom and not have the time to read them to find out mom was lying about the contents. "But does Sara actually know about this? Did you or your dad sit Sara down and talk to her about exactly what was happening?"

"Well, no." He checks his computer screen again. "It doesn't look like it."

I bring both my hands up to stroke my hair back and cradle my head in a brief squeeze. "Here's what I think happened. I think my mom scammed my sister. I think that Sara has no idea that she signed for a second mortgage rather than just putting her name on the existing mortgage, or whatever. I think that all my mom's fancy new toys and bad habits are being funded from this second mortgage, and she decided to have fun before she dies."

Alex sits back in his chair and lets go of the mouse. "Why would she do that?"

"I don't know. She's an old woman who wanted to buy everything she ever wanted before she dies within the next six months and doesn't care about the mess she's leaving behind."

He pulls out two glasses and a golden coloured liquid in an unlabeled bottle from inside the filing cabinet under his desk. "You still drink?"

"Of course."

He pours the amber into the glasses half way up. After Alex hands me the glass he asks, "you're mom's dying?"

So he doesn't know. "Ya. Lung cancer from all those cigarettes she's smoked. She has less than six months to live."

He shakes his head in disbelief. "How long has she known about this?"

One long drink empties my glass. He fills it back up; further than he had the last time. "No idea, but I got told a few weeks ago."

"So she might've conned us all. They didn't get the insurance so when she dies the mortgage is on Sara. Unless she has a will, all her estate would go to your father. That would include the mortgage money in her bank account. Can you get Sara to press charges?" I hadn't thought about that detail. There would be no salvaging the money after she dies. Dad would never give it up.

"Maybe," I initially say positively, but a moment's thought make me recant it. "Probably not."

"Well, we can't do anything since you're not really here, and nothing is confirmed. You'll have to get Sara to do something about it." He tells me.

"And if she doesn't want to press charges?" I remark in a defeated fashion.

"Confront your mom and get her to turn over whatever money she has left. The rest is on you guys when she dies."

"So maybe it's still salvageable." I delude about asking Alex to transfer everything from mom's account from her email. Then imagine finding my way onto her banking online to transfer it that way. The first image may be easier to accomplish. I know for certain that mom has her email automatically login from her laptop. I'm not even sure if there is an online banking for this small family owned bank; I doubt it.

"That's saying that Sara doesn't actually know what's happened. Do you honestly think your mom would do all that?" He doesn't fully believe our conversation. I wouldn't either, if my mother was a regular loving mom; like the stereotypical mom you see on kids shows.

"Yes. And, I can almost guarantee Sara doesn't know. I asked Sara why her name was on the mortgage letter, and she said mom added her. I grabbed the statement later and saw the amount. I figured I'd get a better response out of you than if I had confronted my mother." Then I took the letter so mom wouldn't find it and realize it had been opened.

"Once a bitch always a bitch, eh?" Alex puts his glass in the air to clink against mine.

"Cheers." I tap his glass and take a large couple gulps.

"So what are you going to do now?" He asks.

"Nothing until Sara gets off work. I'll go pick her up and talk to her on the ride home. We'll go from there." I imagine it's going to be one long stressful night.

"Until, then?"

I shrug while thinking it over. "Finish my drink and catch up with an old friend."

He hoists his drink up in a faux glass tapping. Alex finishes his beverage and replaces the contents. Reaching over to my cuddled glass he tops it up. "You can guess how my life's been. Graduated, and the next day I was here. And, every Monday to Friday since. I don't have a life outside working. Stopped hanging out with the guys. My life changed but theirs didn't."

"I lost contact with everyone too." I commiserate

"No offense but you left everyone behind." His statement is a fair jab.

"I did, and didn't. I tried keeping in contact, but like you said, my life changed but theirs didn't. It's hard to keep contact with high school friends once you no longer have anything in common." Everyone I've talked with has said the same thing. The most I've heard was one girl had stayed friends with two friends out of the group she hung out with in high school.

"I live in the same town and couldn't stay in contact." He points out.

"It's hard. Harder when you don't even have a chance of running into them randomly. Phone calls do it at first but then it dies down as old friends are replaced with new ones." I trail off of my excuse and transition into my summarized life. "I graduated and left as soon as I could. Everything I had saved up bought me a plane ticket to Calgary, and bought me a few months to find a job with McDonalds, and go to school. Then I got a job in marketing. I quickly moved up. I have a fiancé. She's amazing."

"Your life sounds like it's everything you could ever want." A touch of jealousy scratches his words.

"It *was* great. And, then I got a call pleading me to come back here. It was the first I had heard from Sara in about a year. I got work to let me work remotely while I deal with family problems." And, it's been drama ever since. I add in my head.

"So you uprooted everything to come back and help your mom."

"I came back because of Sara. Mom is the reason I had to leave." I clear my throat. "Thanks for the drink. I really should get going."

In one gulp, I finish the rest of the drink causing a lingering heat in my throat.

"Right, it was great catching up with you. Talk to Sara and let me know how it turns out. If she doesn't press charges I still might be able to do something." My thoughts turn to the illegal actions he could take, but there might be legal actions he could still take.

"Great, thank you." My best and brightest smile flashes him despite how I feel on the inside.

"Have a great day. Say hi for me."

"Same, say hi to your dad. Bye." The cold chill embraces me like ice cream against a warm spoon. I sink right in, but quickly freeze to the same temperature. The outside reflects how I feel in the inside; numb.

After everything she's ever done, after everything I've done to forget, nothing has changed.

I need my support, my angel who can lead me through this darkness.

I open up my car, and climb inside. Propping up to straighten my torso and thighs, so I can retrieve my phone. Her number is the first one in my text list. I press the phone symbol and the phone dials her number for me.

"Hello?" A male voice answers.

"Hi. Is Lainey there?" I ask a little bewildered at a man answering the phone.

"She's taking a shower. Can I take a message?" My heart starts beating faster at the implications of his words.

"Just tell her to call her fiancé ASAP, please." I say.

"Fiancé? Who's her fiancé?" My eye brows rise with the alarms going off in my head.

"I am, Kara. Who are you?"

"Clayton, I'm her boyfriend."

A solid mass clumps in my chest next to my palpitating heart. "No, she's a lesbian; straight up lesbian. She told me she has no interest in men."

"For fuck sakes." He murmurs away from the phone. When he returns the phone to his mouth he sounds irritated. "That's not what she was saying a half hour ago, or for the last year." He pauses for a moment. "So, she's been cheating on me with a girl."

"She's been cheating on me with a man." I

reverse his statement with no other words I can think at this moment.

"I've got to go deal with this." His voice could cut granite. "Still want to leave a message?"

"Yes, tell her to get her shit out of my apartment."

"Will do." He hangs up.

I pull the phone away from my ear to just stare in bewilderment of what just happened. Did that really just happen?

It occurs to me that I should have asked him if he had any STDs. Or, ask him how serious their relationship is. Or ask him where they were. If they had ever been to our apartment. If they had sex in our bed.

A million questions rush through my head in a light headed haze, none as important as the question of why she had done this.

Tears warm my chilled cheeks. My throat releases a wail. Heart thrashes and beats against my solid chest.

How could she do this to me? Why wasn't I enough?

After all of this stress and news, I break down into an ugly cry. A small part of me looks around suspiciously on occasion to see if anyone is around who might see me.

A knock shocks my heart, and makes my body jump. The ceiling impacts against my head.

My own face stares back at me. She opens the door. "What's wrong?"

"Aren't you supposed to be working?" My attempt at redirection fails.

"Alex called the diner and said you were crying in your car."

Traitor. Mustering up my harshest glare at the bank I tell Sara to, "get in." Alex has forced this conversation to happen early. I haven't had time to prepare what I'll say to her yet.

She runs around the front of the car, and files herself into the passenger seat. The suspense gets to her before I can say anything. "So?" She pressures.

There is easy way to say this. I try the blunt honesty way. "Lainey has been cheating on me with a man. Just found out when I tried to call her because I think mom has been trying to screw you over."

Sara interjects. "We all know she likes to screw us over. But, are you okay? I'm sorry. That has to be rough."

I force myself to look her in the eye as I shake my head. "You don't understand. I was talking with Alex and was mad so I wanted to call her.

So, that's part of it. But, mom." I take a deep breath in to try to make this sound as coherent as possible. "Did you think you were signing your name to be on the existing mortgage, or did you think you were buying the house from mom for two hundred grand?"

"What?" Her question answers my own.

"Mom had you sign papers for you to buy the house from her. She got two hundred thousand dollars as a second mortgage in her bank account from you, and you get the house and remaining payment when she dies." I explain everything the best I understand it. I hand her over the mortgage statement.

She looks over the wording printed on the page. "What? That makes no sense."

"I know." I'm relieved at her understanding.

"Why wouldn't she just pay off the mortgage out of what she got?"

She doesn't get it. "She's buying whatever she wants and hoarding the money. When she dies, she's still married to dad with no will, so all her money goes to him. You'll get stuck with two hundred grand in debt and a mortgage you can't pay for."

"Are you fucking kidding me?" I mentally cheer at her reaction, because the rage is what I'm looking for.

"Alex said you can try to press charges against her." I provide her an out using the option I would take.

"I can't send mom to jail for her last living months." The urge to slap her has never been stronger.

"There isn't much of an option. Alex said we might be able to prove fraud, but you need to bring it up and press charges."

"I'm not going to." Sara interrupts and shuts me down before I can suggest we walk into the bank right now.

"Do you know how serious this is?" I ask.

"Yes, Kara. I'm not an idiot. I can't send mom to jail with everything she's done for me." I don't understand her point and where she's coming from. She should be looking at what mom's done for her but to her.

Sara sounds crazy.

"She's done this to you. Do you not realize that you could lose Caitlyn over this? Mom dies, then the bank wants mortgage payments from you, and when you can't pay they will take the house. You'll lose Caitlyn because the moment Cody finds out you're homeless he's going to go to the judge and label you unfit to mother Caitlyn." I use the only leverage I think will make her budge; her fear of losing her daughter.

"Then I'll talk to dad. He'll give me the money."

"Fat chance." I huff. The greedy bastard wouldn't pass up all that free money. "You need to press charges or you need to confront mom and get her to pay down the mortgage with whatever she hasn't already spent. You're on the hook for the rest." I refuse to tell her that I will help pay it.

"Then I'll do that. I'm not sending mom to jail. I owe her too much." Sara says with stubbornness only she could garner.

There is no point in arguing further. I got one of the options Alex and I had figured out. It may not be the optimum choice but it is something. "Fine."

"I have to get back to work."

"I'll drive you." I offer.

"It's two minutes away. I'll walk." Sara swings open the door to get out. The slam depicts her anger.

I'm upset, and I've pissed her off. She'll forgive me by the time five minutes have passed once she returns home.

Both of us are going to need wine, chocolate, and pizza tonight. Shouldn't be hard to sneak them by mom and hide in our room for the night.

Chapter 4

She's here. – Sally

Her text message is both a relief and terrifying. I wish I could be there to make sure Lainey doesn't rob me blind. The best I was able to do was get my neighbour, Sally, to spy for her arrival and watch over her collection.

Thanks. Make sure you get her key, and let me know what she's taking. I bought practically everything in there so she should only have personal items like clothes, and bathroom stuff. Nothing from the dresser on the right side of the bed. – Kara

The three dots appear immediately. I stare at the phone waiting for the message to come in.

I'll let you know. –Sally

She eases my worries by only a smidgen, but it's enough to get me through the next few minutes with my phone in my pocket.

I brush through the door. The elderly woman stands there at the counter, yelling back to the kitchen to keep order of all the requests.

Mrs. Whitter greets me with a smile, "Good morning Kare. What can I get for you?"

She trips up my welcome. I was going to ask her how she is and receive the same sentiments, but she cut right to business. "Good morning. Three breakfast sandwiches please." I flash a charming smile.

"You, Sara, and your mom." She lists off the assumed people who will be eating the ordered food.

"Caitlyn." I correct, then clarify. "Me, Sara and Caitlyn. Thank you."

"Coming right up." She writes a bunch of scribbles onto her note pad. "Ten bucks."

I hand her a ten dollar bill, and walk to the pick-up line. Other people grab their brown bagged orders one by one as their names are shouted. Patient but not too patiently, I wait for my food.

"Where did you leave my granddaughter this time?" A rough voice whispers close to my ear. I shiver a sordid shiver.

"Hi dad, wrong daughter." Turning to look at him, I notice he too looks older beyond the time passed. More grey hairs in his black hair than he has black, and wrinkles carve his skin. Pounds have been packed on between his gut and his face.

58

"I only have one daughter." He states in a dead cold voice.

My eyes stare despite the urge to roll. "It's Kara."

"No it couldn't be Kara. Kara left us. Might as well be dead. Wouldn't be caught dead back here." If I hadn't grown up with this horrible humour, I wouldn't know he was joking. Doesn't stop the tick of pain in my heart though.

"I'm Kara, and I'm back because of mom; because of Sara." I explain without directly acknowledging his mean joke.

"My daughter wouldn't come back without telling me. She doesn't care about the people who raised her. Doesn't care that she broke her mom's heart when she left; abandoned us. Doesn't care that she's going to hell for marrying a girl." Still hurts dad; still hurts.

In all actuality his jokes are him saying whatever he thinks, but if questioned or rebutted he will swear up and down that he was joking. I know this, but I let him get away with it because, as my father, I owe him that much.

"Kara, you're sandwiches are ready." Thank God Mrs. Whitter interrupts this mind game dad is playing.

I take the bag from Mrs. Whitter and thank her. Turning back to dad, I dismiss myself from the conversation. "Nice chat dad. Have a great day."

His arm reaches out as I lurch to leave. The strong grip holds me in place. The stale coffee breath is prominent as he asks his statement. "No hug for your dear old dad?"

Every bone in my body protests having to hug this man, but I do it because I basically have to. I'm no longer a child, yet he still controls me like I am. I try to hug him quickly but he holds on. I'm at his mercy until he lets go.

Body odor, coffee and gasoline gag my senses until he lets me out of his iron grip.

"Bye." Slightly shamed I walk back out to my car. One song blasted over my speakers cheers me up and gets me home in a better mood. I check my phone for any messages, but there are none. I hope that means all is going well.

Back inside the house is quiet. Mom must still be asleep. Quietly I bound up the stairs.

Little noises muffle through the door. I let myself into the room. Sara and Caitlyn are cuddling on the bed reading a book.

"Breakfast." Presenting the bag to the two of them brings joy and quiet cheers.

Inside the bag are three breakfast sandwiches and a large soup container. Each sandwich is labelled with our names. I hand one to each person as the wrapping dictates.

Inside the soup container is a batch of the hash browns. I'll have to remember to thank Mrs. Whitter the next time I see her. She's always been more than generous to us. Frequently, I have been gifted extra food every other time I've gone into the café.

"Thanks. How long you been up?" Sara says.

"Long enough to get all of this." I bite into my sandwich. I sigh as so many memories of the café flood my senses at the scrumptious taste of English muffin, chipotle mayo, egg, bacon, and tomato. The lettuce has been left off my sandwich in a bid of memory from my high school days. It's a feat for Mrs. Whitter to have remembered that when I don't even remember why I had such a hate for lettuce all those years ago.

I look at each of the other sandwiches to realize Sara and Caitlyn both have varied versions of the original recipe.

Caitlyn has all the vegetables removed, but added cheese. While, Sara had her tomatoes removed.

Caitlyn has decided to forgo her sandwich for the hash browns. I don't blame her for her interest in the buttery potatoes; however I have noticed a tendency for the little girl to eat only the potato portion of a meal, typically in the fry form. It's not exactly healthy but like Sara said, you need to pick your battles.

I've stopped side eyeing the position the two are in. If I've learned anything it's that nothing can remove Caitlyn from Sara's lap when she's sitting. The tiny body becomes an attached limb for the first few days back, made worse only by Sara's return to work each day. Mom has been useless in helping me calm Caitlyn, so I've been the replacement for Sara. My work completion has been practically nonexistent. Still, the most productive parts of my day have been at nap time, but as I carefully work around a sleeping toddler.

Today is Sara's first day off. From what she's told me that's usually the day Caitlyn starts to return to her normal independent self.

"Do you have to work today?" Sara asks just after I take a bite of my food. I raise an eyebrow. She insists on asking me questions right after I shovel food in my mouth. It's becoming an annoying habit.

As much as I would love to spend the day purely playing around with the two of them, I have a bunch of work to do. My Monday to Friday job doesn't line up well with her waitress hours. "Ya, I need to do some catch up."

"Sorry." She looks crushed.

"No, no. It's not a problem. Big project, and not enough time in a day to do it." I explain as an alternative excuse so she doesn't feel bad. "What are you going to do today?"

"We're going to have a We day; all about Caitlyn. Make some cookies, play whatever she wants, watch a movie and cuddle, and whatever else we can think of." Her plans are adorable, and sound just like what Caitlyn needs to reconnect. I should be able to join in on a couple of those things. At the least, I could work while also watching the movie, and take a five minute break to eat some cookies.

I'll try to deal with mom as much as I can, so Sara can spend more time focusing on Caitlyn.

"Awesome. Sounds like a fun day." My phone vibrates so I pull it out of my pocket and read the message.

She's gone, but I think she's going to try to come back. Tried taking everything she could get her hands on but I stopped her. Got Benny to escort her out with just a box of clothes. – Sally

Did you get the key back? – Kara

No, sorry. It was too hectic and I forgot to ask. Not that she would have listened. Benny says he can change the lock for you. – Sally

Thank you for helping with her. I have a feeling I wouldn't of had anything to come back to if you and Benny didn't step in. I'm going to message Benny to get a new lock. Would you mind looking after my plants and fish until I return? - Kara

I wish this was something I could be there for. As much as I would hate the confrontation, at least I could make sure she wasn't stealing from me blindly.

"What's wrong?" Sara asks.

"Lainey's trying to rob me. My neighbour had to get our maintenance guy to escort her out, but she thinks Lainey will come back for more." I quickly decide to send a text to Benny.

Hey, thanks for the help with Lainey. Could you change the lock on my door? – Kara

His answer comes back immediately.

Already started. Talked with Sally. I gave her one key, and I'll hold onto your copy. – Benny

Thanks, you're amazing! – Kara

"That sucks. Do you need to go back home? It sounds like you need to go deal with that."

Part of me wants to jump on the offer, but I know that I'm needed more here. "No, it's fine. I can stay. My maintenance guy is going to change the locks so she can't get in again."

"I'm sorry. I think that is one of the worst things about the breakup, is having to divide your things." A glazed look crosses her eyes. I know she's remembering her break up with Cody.

"There isn't much to divide because I had a full apartment when she moved in. But, she has personal items there. It's not as bad as it could be, but she's trying to take my things now. But, Benny is changing the locks so I won't have to worry anymore." I stop myself. I know I sound dumb and unsure with all the 'buts.' I'm not certain everything will be fine because there are still so many things that could go wrong without me there to oversee things.

I can only hope that Sally and Benny will keep an eye on things until mom dies. I just need her to croak, I'll get all the fires put out, then I'll go home to put my life back together.

Chapter 5

I look on to the trailer Caitlyn should be housed in. I don't mean to judge, but I'm judging; not because of the trailer, but because the state of it.

Snow only does so much to hide the dirt, grim, rust and rot. Bare plywood peaks out from broken siding. One of the windows is taped up with duct tape in three directions. The center of the three looks thicker, as if covering up a hole.

From Sara's stories I wonder if Cody threw something in a fit, and broke the window.

I turn off the car and get out with the medicine in hand.

It's a short trip to the door, but I watch my footsteps the whole way. I wouldn't want to step on anything.

I knock.

Darla answers the door in ratty pajamas. I caught her ill prepared to receive visitors. "What do you want?"

Her attitude grates at me. "Hi, I'm Kara. I'm Sara's sister. I have Caitlyn's medicine."

"What medicine?" She deadpans.

"She has strep throat, and these are her antibiotics. Sara had forgotten to send them with her last night. Sara said she told Cody." I explain.

"Well, no one told me." I stop myself from saying obviously in the same attitude she is giving.

"I could show you what to do. It's a little bit of a process, and Caitlyn should be taking a dosage now." It's not difficult, but I don't want to take any chances, and I need to see my niece.

"Ya, whatever. Come in." She steps aside.

I step into the house, and feel like I should refuse to take off my shoes. The house is grimy and dirty. Black finger prints smudge the light switches and door edge, like they haven't been wiped down in years. Finger oils catch the dust and dirt, and build up over time. It would take a long time to collect so much on the door.

Dishes have piled up so bad there isn't a clear spot on the counter. Not one place setting at the table is available for a meal.

Cat vomit lays dried on the floor amidst kid toys.

I don't know how this can be an acceptable environment for a child. I don't think the family law people would like this environment.

One tiny person is missing. It's early in the morning, so she shouldn't be having nap time. "So, where's Caitlyn?"

"Somewhere."

I hope she's joking. "Where's Cody?"

"Sleeping in the back." She's flippant.

I remove my boots to help her search, but it turns into a search of one as Darla sits down at the kitchen table.

A body shifts on the couch. I barely hold my shriek of surprise. I don't recognize his face. It may be from the amount of dirt and grime, but it may be that I never knew him.

I walk down the long hall. The computer room is empty, but the next door is closed.

Looking back at the girlfriend I see her still sitting at the table.

She's left me to my own devices, so I open the door. My heart drops. Lying on the floor on her stomach is my tiny niece. I leap over to her and pull her up into my arms.

Her cries are a relief. For half a moment I thought she may have been dead. Little arms push me away with her full strength.

I let her pull away just enough for me to look her over. She's in the same clothes we sent her here in. It's a full black outfit for shirt and pants; with a cat silhouette in gold.

Her little body coughs with the strain on her lungs and throat. All throughout her eyes are closed. I have no doubt she doesn't know who I am.

Her pants look round where her diaper is. I poke the front to tell if the diaper is full or not; it is. A small sweep of the area reveals a small stack of diapers, and a carton of wipes.

Caitlyn's tantrum is in full cue, so I grab the diaper and wipes and proceed to try to change her. Her pants are easier to get off than I had thought. Twice a foot manages to kick me in the face.

The diaper comes off almost as Velcro. The stench of her poop hits me as I see it; everywhere. Yellow brown smooshes into the wipe as I pull some of the mess away.

Her squirming isn't helping. She twists and turns. Legs fly with as much strength as she can muster.

I hum an odd, and higher pitched tune. Something that I've seen Sara do to calm her down. It works enough to open her eyes, but backfires when she throws herself to hug me.

Letting her have a moment of comfort, I hug her close. My shirt suffers for the act, but I don't have a care at the moment.

Wailing increases as I peel her away from me to finish the diaper change. Her bum is red from the diaper rash, but I can't do anything about it. She only cooperates enough for me to finish and clothe her again.

"Get the fuck out of my house!" Cody's booming voice scares me.

"It's Kara. Darla let me in for her anti biotics." I search the ground for the forgotten medicine. Standing up I reach to hand them to him.

He takes the bottle. "Get the fuck out of my house or I'll force you out!"

"I just-"

"NOW!" His face darkens to a shade of red. The crazy eyes threaten what his mouth doesn't. I'm scared of what this man could do.

I turn to say good bye to Caitlyn, but my arm is yanked hard out of the room and I'm thrust towards the living room; towards the door.

Caitlyn scream tears me apart. Her cries in a string of "no, no, no" break my heart.

There is nothing I can do.

The force of Cody coming towards me, leads me out the door, and running to my car.

A glass bottle flies by my head and smashes against the ground not far from me. I look over my shoulder at Cody.

"Never come here again!" There's an added threat left unspoken.

Once in the car I start it and go. I don't stop until I get to the crossroads between the way home and down to town.

I don't know what to do. I have to tell Sara. I pull out my cell phone, and dial for the café. She answers straight away. "Thank you for calling-"

"Sara." My voice whimpers her name.

"Kara, what's wrong?"

The whole story comes rushing out of my mouth. "Caitlyn. I went to drop off the medicine and they let me inside to look for her and I found her in her room on the floor, and she was passed out. And, I woke her up and she was crying. And, she was still dressed in the same clothes from last night. And, I don't think they changed her diaper since last night, so I changed her diaper. And then Cody yelled at me to get out of his house. Then he threw a glass bottle at me as I was running to my car. Kara, what do I do? We can't leave Caitlyn there."

There is a long pause. "Did you get any video or pictures?"

"No."

There is a pause seeded deep with defeat. "Then there's nothing we can do."

"Can't we call the cops?" I plead.

"It won't help."

"But she isn't being taken care of, and the house was a filthy mess, and there was some random guy sleeping on their couch." The more the details the better my case may be.

"I know that." She outbursts in her anger, then quietens down. "Kara, none of that is any offense big enough to get her taken away. You call the cops now, and all they're going to do is go to Cody and ask for his side of the story. They can't even go in the house unless immediate danger is suspected. And, Cody's going to say you were trespassing or trying to kidnap Caitlyn, and it's going to cause more problems for me."

"That's bullshit!" I cry in horror.

"I know. But it is what it is, and we can't do anything about it. I should have told you to take pictures and video if something happened, and that's my fault." There is a pause. "Kara, I have to go. Go home and stay home. We'll talk later."

She hangs up without another word.

It's not fair.

My heart pounds and tears fill my eyes. I put the car on the path home.

Pain lets itself out in a whine. Tears fall in heaps from my eyes, and the snot runs from my nose. I hyperventilate as the shock of everything hits me hard.

I feel so helpless and hopeless.

Then there's nothing we can do. That sentence echoes in my head over and over again.

Somehow, I manage to make it home without causing an accident in my full meltdown. I park, and shut the car off.

Anger bubbles up in an action of hitting the steering wheel. My hand hurts where I bashed it, but it takes away some of the pain in my chest.

My tears dry up well enough for me to make it inside, only to be greeted by my mother.

"You should be ashamed of yourself. Sara's going to lose custody of Caitlyn because of you. How could you do that to your own sister?"

"What the fuck are you talking about?" I return, not in the mood for this confrontation.

"Cody called and said he's going to take Sara to court. He has witnesses saying that you tried kidnapping and drugging Caitlyn. He's going to get full custody and Sara is never going to see Caitlyn again. He's pulling a restraining order out against you." Mom looks smug, and not at all concerned.

I can't take this right now. It hardens everything inside me. "Where are the police then? I'll go talk to them right now. Tell them how he assaulted me after his girlfriend let me in. How he threw a glass bottle at my head. I'll get a restraining order against him and tell the court everything I saw. I'll call child protective services on him. I will make his life a living hell. How about that? How about you tell him that since you are so buddy buddy with him? I have just as much evidence in what happened as he does. I hate him, and I hate you."

It's not the first time I've talked back and yelled at my mother, but the number isn't too far off from that. She walks away from me, because she has nothing more to say. My position was made clear to her. How much I despise her and Cody at this moment cannot be put into better words.

The anger dispels all other feelings and takes over. There has to be something I can do. The rest of my day is made up for me. I'll scour the internet for solutions.

Chapter 6

Never had I imagined our house could be so quickly filled with uninvited people. The news broke about mother's death moments after Sara called the medical team.

The neighbours, Mr. and Mrs. Teisen, were here not one minute later. The medical team arrived after five more people set up shop in our living room.

Sara was a mess, so I took over discussing the circumstances with James Wilson while the elder paramedic took care of the body.

I spoke with the sheriff, so Sara didn't have to. Told him I had found her, when Sara was actually the one who discovered she had passed away in her sleep.

Sara exchanged happy stories with people. She wept and cried, and mourned her loss. My feelings have been more equated to numbness. I'm not happy or sad. For me, the loss is that of not having a functioning happy mother, but I'd mourned that for my whole life.

Half the town has been in and out. We have enough casseroles to last us a year. Many have declared their doubts of our ability to cook and take care of ourselves at this time.

I've taken the condolences, and the 'we're so glad you made it back to spend her last days with her.' But, I feel nothing.

Perhaps it makes me a monster.

I can't and won't dwell on such thoughts right now. Death is handled by everyone in vastly different ways. More so when you didn't have a great relationship with such a vital person in your life.

I stand at an impromptu funeral setting they declared a wake. Mother is in her bed, and people are taking their turns viewing the body to say their good byes. Others are saying their eulogies in the living room.

One person is noticeably missing after I zone back in. At the edge of the room I easily sneak out without anyone knowing.

Her shoes are still here, so I know she didn't go outside. She doesn't have many places to hide; less because she refuses to enter mom's room.

I enter the kitchen first. Only one woman is present, and she isn't my sister. It takes a moment of staring at this stranger to recognize her as the library mouse. "Lynn, hi."

Her expression turns to shock, then the uncomfortable look of empathy people express when dealing with those left behind after death. She rushes over to me and hugs me really tight. "I'm sorry about your mom. I know you two never really got along, but it still sucks to lose a parent."

I try to remember if either of her parents has passed away, but I don't remember anything like that. She sounds like she's experienced a parent dying, but I feel awkward enough to refuse to ask.

"Thank you." I reflexively answer.

"I had heard you'd come back to town, but I hadn't seen you." Lynn quietly moves on from the awkward silence I left.

"Ya, to help Sara with mom. I've been working from home. I don't get out of here much." I go grocery shopping, and give rides to Sara for work. There isn't much else that requires me to leave.

"Makes sense. So I suppose you'll be leaving soon then; after the funeral." She sounds dejected.

"I hadn't really thought about it. I thought there would be about four more months before she passed. I'll probably stay as long as my work lets me to help Sara deal with all the fall out. Speaking of Sara, have you seen her?"

"She went upstairs." Lynn points to where the stairs should be through the wall. "She was trying to call someone."

"Thank you. I should check on her. I was trying to find her." I explain as an excuse to leave.

"Of course." She leans in and pecks my lips. "Give me a call if you want to talk."

"Sure." I answer a bit in shock. Lynn leaves the room before I realize I had deleted her number long ago.

Shaking off the surprise, I return to my mission.

Half up the stairs I can hear her sobbing.

She's in our room clenching Caitlyn's favourite blanket. It occurs to me that neither Cody nor Caitlyn have made an appearance. Neither has dad for that matter, but I don't think this is about him.

Wrapping my arms around her I try to comfort her the only way I know how, despite knowing nothing will help her.

"What happened?"

"Cody." She sobs. I give her time to continue

when she can. "He says I can't have Caitlyn. Said mom should have picked my week with her to die. He won't even let me talk to her."

That's cold hearted. I have nothing I can say to her, so I hold her tighter.

Sara is a wreck.

I think it's for the best because Caitlyn wouldn't understand all of this, but I won't tell Sara that. We can set the funeral for when Caitlyn is home and emotions aren't so raw.

I'll sit and hold her for as long as she needs me to. Until long after my limbs have tingled then fallen asleep. Until my back aches from this twisted angle.

Chapter 7

I open the door to give them a piece of my mind for ringing the doorbell a bunch of times in the middle of the night. Until, I see the sheriff. A cold chill rushes into my bones. I might as well be staring at the reaper himself.

"What's going on?" My voice is deep and scratchy from sleep.

"Are you Sara?"

"Sara? Ya, no. I'm Kara." Half way through talking my brain starts waking up. "Come in."

I leave him to let himself inside while I wake Sara up. My heart pumps adrenaline through my body because this can only be something about one of two people; Caitlyn or dad. I believe the former since he specifically asked for Sara.

I crawl onto the bed to reach her over pressed against the wall. Hand on her arm I shake her awake. She tries to roll over, but can't. "Sara, the sheriff is here and asking for you. I think it's something about Caitlyn."

Her eyes open the moment her sleep hazed

mind hears the name of her baby. In her bid to jump up and race downstairs she knocks me in the jaw. I fall over from the force.

Once I recover, I quickly go down the stairs myself and rush to hear what is happening.

"The bruising was abnormal, and consistent with an assault. Child protective services were called as they would in all cases like this. Once the doctors release her, she will be in their custody, and presumably returned to you once you've been cleared."

Sara is on the couch, tears streaming down her cheeks and mouth open. I let myself breathe again when I hear that she's alive. "What happened?" I ask.

The sorrowful expression hardens a little. He probably hates having to make these sorts of calls as much as people hate receiving them. "Caitlyn was brought to the medical center when she was found unresponsive with a high fever. They were able to stabilize her and bring her to the hospital. However, in the examination the doctors noticed immense bruising all over her body."

"She, Caitlyn had strep throat. I gave Cody the medication. Did he not give it to her and the virus got worse, or was the fever from brain trauma?" I ask because the differences between the two matter.

He shakes his head slightly. "I don't have that information."

"So what do we need to do?" I ask.

"I want to go to the hospital. I want to see Caitlyn." Sara makes to get up from the couch, but is stopped by the sheriff holding his hand out in a gesture to hold her from across the room.

"I need to ask you a few questions first." He pulls out his note pad and a pen. "When was the last time you saw Caitlyn?"

"Five days ago, when Cody picked her up for his turn. Kara saw her four days ago. She had to drop off the medicine. I forgot to give it to Cody." Sara explains.

"And how did she seem?" The sheriff pushes further to me.

"It was a mess. She was a mess. I went to the house and Darla let me in. I found Caitlyn in her room on the floor. She was sleeping. I changed her diaper, which didn't look like it had been done since she had left us. She was coughing. She cried the whole time I was there. Cody threw me out of his house and threatened me. Said he would press charges for trespassing and get a restraining order." The sheriff writes down everything I say.

He turns back to my sister. "Sara, do you have any reason to believe Cody might hurt Caitlyn?"

She laughs hysterically and shakes her head. "Of course, but no one fucking listened to me. They said *oh well* and handed her to him. He's got a fucking temper and beat me. He raped me. He stabbed me. He throws things all the time when he's angry or frustrated. He scares me to death. But no one listened to me and now my baby's going to die." A hysterical fit of crying nearly makes the last sentence unrecognizable.

Seeing my sister in the midst of a complete breakdown I get the sheriff's attention. "Are we done? Can I take her to see Caitlyn now?"

"Yes." He flips pages in his notepad until he finds what he's looking for. The page is ripped out and handed to me. "Name of the hospital, doctor information, room number, is all there. I will call ahead to allow you in. You will be escorted in and under surveillance."

He leads the way out. At the door he says in hushed tones to, "come down to the station tomorrow to fill out a report on your encounter."

"Okay."

"Drive safe. Watch out for animals on the road." He says as he walks to his car.

"Will do. Thank you." I close the door and go back to the edge of the living room.

Sara is on the couch crying. I leave her there to deal with gathering necessities. Up to our room I grab Caitlyn's diaper bag, her blanket and a stuffed animal. I put on a sweater and socks, and change into jeans. I grab Sara socks and a sweater. There are doubts that she'll be coherent enough to put on her boots, never mind everything else.

Taking my load down to the door, I put everything but Sara's clothes into my car. Back in the living room is a changed Sara. Her eyes are still wet from the tears, but they are unmoving. Her expression is dead. I think she's either in shock or broken from the past few days.

"Sara? We're going to get you dressed, and then go out to the car. I've got everything ready, and we're going to go see Caitlyn." I say as sweetly as I can. She doesn't look at me, but she gets up and goes to the door. She misses her boots and just walks out of the house and to my car. I grab everything left, including her boots, and leave after her.

Chapter 8

"Dough ball!" Caitlyn cries cheerfully. One tiny activity of making cinnamon buns has everyone present beaming with the first thread of happiness they've been able to grasp in a long time.

Between mom passing away, Caitlyn's hospital stay, the funeral, and dealing with the estate, none of us have had much time to be cheerful.

My phone buzzes. I look at the notification and see that Mouse has texted me. A goofy grin cracks my face with the warm feelings that bubble up.

"Ohhh, is that your new girlfriend." Sara teases.

"Shut up." I reprimand myself as soon as the defensive words leave my mouth. "I mean shush. Bad Auntie."

"Sooo?" She drags out the word to emphasize the question she isn't asking, but desperately wishes to.

"She's not my girlfriend. I have to go back home eventually; you know." We had this talk last night when I asked Sara for Lynn's phone number.

"You could always move back here." She's made her point very clear that she won't move with me, and I've made my point that I wouldn't move back permanently. It won't stop her from trying. I raise my eyebrow in defiance. "Fine. But that doesn't mean she couldn't be your girlfriend while you're here, and maybe more; maybe longer." The eyebrow wag makes me chuckle. I pluck a small piece of dough out from around the edge of the ball and toss it at her.

"Bad Auntie. No throw." Caitlyn's tiny lips are pursed out, and her eyebrows are scrunched. She's making her angry face, but it's so adorable.

"You're right, Auntie shouldn't throw food. I'm sorry." I apologize to her.

"You better be sorry with how long this stuff takes to make. You know I could have been to the store and back with cinnamon buns by now; like ten times." Sara complains.

"But it's so much better homemade, and we can put anything we want in it." She's being dramatic. We haven't even started any of the waiting times. I go over the recipe again. I want to make sure we didn't forget anything.

86

Kara Walker

3 cups House Temperature Water

1/3 cup Oil

½ cup Honey

2 Eggs

1 tsp Salt

7 to 8 cups of All Purpose Flour

2 tbsp Yeast

Add in order and stir at each addition. Best stirred by hand after flour addition. *Flour hands before handling dough.

Let rise in saran wrapped, flour lined bowl 15 min. Punch down.

Repeat rising step.

Roll out dough to desired thickness.

Fill with fillings.

Roll and cut to desired size.

Bake 350 degrees for 15-20 min.

It all seems to be in order. We've remembered all the ingredients. The dough ball is sticky, but not too sticky. I think we've got a good consistency of flour to wet. It ended up taking about seven and a half cups of flour. But, that's why the recipe says somewhere between seven and eight cups of flour.

I plop the dough ball into the bowl and Sara wraps the top.

My hands are covered in dough. I can feel the pressure of the portions under my nails. I had forgotten to flour my hands before and during my handling of the dough.

I wash the sticky, gooey dough from my hands, but I feel like I'll never get it all off.

"So what are we putting in it." Sara puts her hands on her hips. I don't know if she was asking me, or just Caitlyn. She is looking at Caitlyn, so I don't say anything.

"Apple." Caitlyn gleefully suggests.

"Apple cinnamon cinnamon buns." I declare.

"Does it really need the second cinnamon?" Sara questions.

"I don't know." Each word and pause is dragged out thoughtfully. "They're cinnamon buns, and we are putting apple cinnamon filling in them. So, that would make them apple cinnamon cinnamon buns? Or, would that make them apple cinnamon buns."

"I don't know. I think you just need the one cinnamon."

"I'm gonna go with both." I decide.

She puffs out loud air. "That's just because

you like saying cinnamon."

"It's a fun word to say." I shrug. I switch the conversation a little to get us back on track. "So, now we wait fifteen minutes, toss it around a little, wait another fifteen minutes, and then we can get to the filling."

Sara groans in protest. "Seriously, I could walk to the store and back faster than that."

"But would they have apple cinnamon cinnamon buns?" I ask seriously.

Caitlyn coughs. Her little body shakes a couple times before she announces her pain. "Oww."

My smile drops a little, knowing the pain is from her bruised body.

Sara frowns. "I know baby. I'm sorry."

I try to put my hand on Sara's arm, but she pushes me away. Sara walks out of the kitchen.

"Mommy has to go potty. How about we put on an Olie Olie Olie?" I cheerfully announce.

"Olie Olie Olie." She echoes in excitement. "Upidy." Caitlyn reaches her arms up so I can take her off of the table. I set her in front of the television and start a recording of Rolie Polie Olie.

She's settled and cheery with the theme song

playing. Now, to find my sister and put out this fire.

Sara is in our bedroom with tears down her cheeks. She isn't sobbing, so that's at least a plus. I hug her to let her know I'm here for her.

Sara breaks down, and one whine is released. She breaks away from me. "You've seen it. I can't stand it. My baby is broken because I couldn't stop the judge from awarding half custody to that asshole. I knew, I didn't know, but I knew something would happen. He raped me, assaulted me, assaulted other girls, and beat up the guys while drunk. He's got anger issues. He has random lowlife friends who come over. Any one of them could have- He does drugs, and he's an alcoholic. And, those fucking law people wouldn't take any of it into consideration when they handed him my baby. My baby, I can't believe- She always cried. She cried when he would hold her as a newborn. She would cry when he would take her off to go with him. She never wanted this. I never wanted this. She's my baby. She's half his DNA, but she's mine. He tried to kill her by pushing me down stairs while I was pregnant. I should have left. I should have put an unknown father on her birth certificate and ran away. I had thought about it, but stupidly thought I could make it work. It's not fair. Why did they have to give him custody because he asked? It's not fair. My poor baby."

No one should ever have to go through this. I keep my mouth shut because the only thing I can think of at this moment is that it could have been worse. That wouldn't help.

But, I have to say something. "At least he's in custody; being questioned. You have temporary full custody of her. When the judge finds out what happened, he won't get her back."

"Maybe. Maybe not. What if they don't find enough evidence? It's not like she's old enough to tell them what happened."

"Then we take it from there." I reason. "At this point, there is nothing more that we can do except go downstairs and be with her."

"Okay. I need some time to cool down." Sara wipes both eyes of her tears.

"Okay. I'll watch her. Take your time." I start walking out of the room, but I stop to look back. "Just don't miss filling time because you might not like what I put in the rolls." I walk out.

"No raisins!" She shouts after me.

Chapter 9

I wake up. I can't figure out why, but my heart is pumping. I don't remember my dream so I could have had a nightmare that woke me. Turning over I knock into Sara a little. A bit adjusting gets me settled. I try to go back to sleep.

It doesn't work. Whether my mind doesn't let me fall back asleep, or my heart; I don't know. Either way, it's frustrating. I roll over. Maybe a different position will help. I look behind me, and carefully move. I get my elbow under me, and prop myself up rolling from the side of my foot to my heel.

My ear perks up to the sound of our stairs squeaking. I swear I can hear someone shushing right after.

I freeze completely. Did that just happen? Did I really hear something? There isn't any noise after that. No one is there, and no one is coming upstairs. It's an old house. It makes noises sometimes; strange noises.

Did Sara lock the door when I asked her to?

I roll back down to my side. I need to make sure that there's nothing there if I'm ever going to get back to sleep.

Quietly, just in case, I slowly roll to the edge and swing my legs over. Sliding to the ground I make sure not to make a noise, nor wake the two people in the bed. Once upright, I slowly creep over towards the door. By the time I get to the other side of the bed, something sets off the twinkling music of one of Caitlyn's toys downstairs.

"Turn it off! You'll wake them up." Someone distinctly whisper yells. I freeze again. I think they do the same downstairs. My heart races. There is someone downstairs, and they don't want to wake us up. At best guess they are just trying to rob us. Momentarily, I think about shutting the door and barricading ourselves in the room, but I'm not sure I could do that fast enough to beat them coming upstairs and into our room.

I wait.

"Get over here." Creaking goes down the stairs.

I wait.

No one starts coming upstairs again. I open the door a crack to hear better. I try to remember that if I can hear them better here, they can hear me better. If I can get Sara up we might be able to barricade ourselves in the room in time.

Careful not to make any noise myself, I go two steps to Sara. How do I do this? I decide to shake her awake lightly.

"Wh" I slap my hand over her mouth and turn my head to the side. By looking at the door I hope that no one heard any of that. Fear hits me as I realize I should have shut the door before I went to wake her up.

In a bit more urgency I lean down, and whisper as quietly as I can. "Someone broke in." Her eyes are wide when I pull away from her ear. I take my hand off her mouth to put my finger up to my mouth.

She looks to her side where her baby girl is still soundly sleeping. Sara pulls her hand out of the covers and makes a hang loose signal. I put up both my hands up and shrug. I have no idea what she is trying to tell me.

She puts the hand back into the hang loose signal, but puts it up to her face; thumb to ear and pinky to mouth. Phone. Where's my phone?

Downstairs charging on the kitchen table. Then I remember mom has a phone in her room.

Turning around in spot, I tiptoe to the door. Peering around the door frame I pull back when I see a dark figure near the front door.

I don't hear anyone come up the stairs, so I try looking again. The figure is still there, but I don't think he can see me here. He may not be looking at me.

I have to get across the hall. Dropping down I decide to take the risk and crawl across the hall. If I stick to the back of the hall he won't be able to see me at any angle. Mom's door might be an issue.

Crawling proves to be louder than I thought. The fabric of my sleeping pants scraps against the carpet. I take my chance and roll back onto my feet. I crawl on the tips of my feet, and with my hands. The cuffs drag on the floor a bit.

I look down to the main floor; as much as I can see. Managing to make it across the hall all the way. Reaching up to the door handle I grab onto it like a lifeline. Painfully slow I turn the door knob. Something so quick that takes a split second normally, takes around a minute.

When the door knob won't turn anymore, I pause and listen. All the small noises seem far away. Moving the door a couple inches open I take just as long to turn the door knob back to its original position. One deep breath in then in a fluid movement, I open the door and crawl inside the room. The process is repeated to close the door quietly.

I stand up the moment I am done.

Her phone is beside her bed. There isn't as much light in this room, so when I get to the table I fumble around a little until I find the phone. I press the Talk button and listen. There is a dial tone.

I press number two. It auto dial's the emergency police line, aka Sheriff Coller's personal cell phone. It rings four times, before going to voicemail. "It's Kara. People have broken into our house. Sara, Caitlyn and I are trapped. Help us please." I pause at the end before hanging up. I don't know what to say. I try the medical hotline on speed dial number one.

"Hello?" It's James Wilson. He sounds like I interrupted him in the middle of a good joke. He's stifling his laughter.

"Oh my god! It's Kara. Someone's broken in. You have to help us. I can't get a hold of the sheriff." I whisper.

"What? I'm sorry you have to speak up." I don't know how much he is able to hear.

I speak as loud as I dare. "Help! It's Kara. We need help. People broke into the house."

"Who? Who's in your house?" His voice turns serious in an instant.

"I don't know. I can't reach the sheriff. I can't talk. We need help."

"Okay. I'm going to try to help. Stay where you are. If you can, get out of the house and get somewhere safe. I'm going to the Coller's house then we will be there in a few minutes."

"Thank you." Is the only reply I give him before I hang up. I wait a few seconds. There are no footsteps up the stairs.

I need to get back to Sara. Then we can barricade ourselves in her room. Wait. Windows. I can go to a window. Maybe get an idea about who is doing this. Unless they walked of course. That brings a chilling thought. It's probably someone we know. Who else could it be? Why would someone drive two hours here to break into some random house near the furthest point up the mountain? Who would do that and know that we are sleeping upstairs.

I slink over to the wall facing the front of the house. Sure enough through the blind slats I see a white truck running just outside. There are a few people in town with that truck, but the first one that pops into my mind is Cody. That's a scary thought. He can be violent. He not only has motive to just steal, but-

I don't want to go there. We have to try to get out of here.

Staying hidden upstairs isn't an option. I don't think a barricaded door would stop him either. We need to do something while he still thinks

we're asleep. While they think we are asleep.

My car keys are downstairs. All our boots are downstairs. We need to leave but the only door is blocked. We could try to escape out a window. The one in this room would be best. The window behind the bed would work best. It's the only one that doesn't face the front of the house. We wouldn't have to risk someone coming out at the same time we try to jump.

I walk back to the door and open it. Sara is standing at our room's door staring back at me. Caitlyn is in her arms. I make a come here motion, and then hold my hands out like I do when getting Caitlyn to come to me. Sara needs to crouch, so it would be easier to have Caitlyn come by herself.

Sara says something I can't hear to Caitlyn. She puts Caitlyn on the ground. She kisses her head and lets her go.

I lean down a bit, and hold out my hands for Caitlyn. She toddles over to me without making more than a tiny stomping noise. When I grab her up I kiss her cheek.

Sara learned from me, and crawls over on her hands and feet. We go deeper inside the room. Sara shuts the door so that it's almost closed behind her.

"We need to escape." Caitlyn reaches out for

Sara, and whines a bit. I immediately hand her over to keep her quiet.

"What? How the hell are we going to do that?" She seems angry at me.

I point behind me. "Out the window. James was going to the sheriff's house first to wake him up, and then they were going to head over here. But we don't have enough time to wait."

"They haven't come up here yet. Maybe they won't. We should just shut the door and throw everything we can at it."

I didn't want to tell her, but I don't think we have time to argue about whether we escape or stay. We don't have time for that. "I think it's Cody. It looks like his truck outside. He's not going to stop just because the door is blocked."

"I need to get her in warmer clothes. It's too cold out there for her." She makes a move to put Caitlyn in my arms, but I don't let her.

"We'll lower her in a blanket and carry her in that. She'll be fine. We don't have time to get warmer clothes. I've got bare feet you think I'm going to last long out there? We'll run to their truck. It's running. They won't have locked the doors. We take that and drive off." I'm not too sure of the plan myself, but I don't let her argue further. I go to the window and slide it open. It looks really far down, but I can't really think about that. People have jumped from higher and survived, right?

It's cold out. It's only going to get colder once I hit the snow.

Crawling up on the bed I think about how I'm going to do this. I should get as close to the ground as possible. Turning around, I brace myself with the side of the window while I position myself on my knees on the window sill.

I don't want to do this, but I can't let that stop me.

With both hands now beside my knees, I put my weight on them and start to lower my lower half of my body out of the window. There isn't anything that I can brace myself on. I try to get a grip on the siding, but that seems useless. The initial dropping sensation terrifies me, but not as much as when my hands lose their grip and I fall the rest of the way to the ground. My feet hurt first. They slide out from underneath me, and hit against the house. My whole body stings for a moment.

I stay quiet. I hope no one heard anything.

I don't think anything is broken. Maybe we should have tried getting some warmer clothes; at least something for our feet. Getting up is just as hard as it was to leap out of the window, but now there is pain.

Sara looks worried before she disappears from the window. She's gone a couple moments.

What's happening?

Hoping we didn't get caught already. She soon appears with Caitlyn bundled in the blanket. It looks like Sara put Caitlyn in the middle of the blanket and grabbed the four edges. She lowers the bundle until she is only gripping the four corners. It isn't enough to get Caitlyn in my arms by she is within reach.

"I've got her." I say up to Sara. We've gone this far. She can't argue. I don't get a warning, but my body didn't seem to need one. Caitlyn is in my arms. She's whining like she's about to full out cry. I sink to the ground with her, and search for her with in the blankets. Once I uncover her head, she looks at me like I betrayed her. Her lips are pouted. I kiss her forehead, and whisper to her. "It's okay. I've got you. You just have to be quiet for a couple more minutes."

I rearrange her blankets to almost swaddle her. It's a large bundle, but I get her set up in my arms. Unsteady, I stand up using the house as a bit of a support.

Looking up at Sara; she's panicking and waving at me. She mouth's something that I'm sure was the word go. She points behind the neighbour's house, and then disappears.

She closes the window.

Was she caught? Or did she just hear something?

Just in case she was caught I run behind the house with Caitlyn. They might look out the window.

The world is quiet.

Caitlyn starts whimpering again, so I rock her to comfort her. I shift the blanket around her a bit more to cover more of her head. Now when I put her against me her face would be mostly covered from the elements.

I don't know how long I wait for her nor how long I should wait. Whoever is in the house might have found her, or she could be biding her time after hearing a noise. I don't know. Either way, what would she want me to do?

That's easy. Make sure Caitlyn is safe.

Whatever happens to her, she would want Caitlyn safe.

I don't know how far away the sheriff is. Should I take the truck and run? Or should I put Caitlyn in the truck and try to save Sara? What about the neighbours? There has to be someone that could help. It's not like the whole town is involved with this. If it's Cody then his accomplices should be his friends. None of them live near us. Our neighbours should be fine. I can keep Caitlyn there until the sheriff arrests them.

Right next door isn't far, and they have a back door. Getting up from the ground, I trudge through the snow and get to the Teisen's back door. I check the door handle. The door opens. For courtesy sake I ring the doorbell a few times. Maybe that will wake them before I have to scare them awake.

Walking inside, I lock the door behind me. They have a deadbolt, that I'm sure has never been used before. When the warm inside encompasses me it causes everything to burn. I hope Caitlyn doesn't have any of the same feelings. It would be worse for her than for me. She's so small.

She doesn't make any noises, and she's alert, so I don't think she's had any harm. Nearly jogging I get to the front door and lock it. The hallway light turns on behind me. It scares me first.

"Turn around slowly or I'll shoot." Mr. Teisen's voice booms behind me.

I turn slowly. Mr. Teisen stands with his shot gun pointed our way. "Help us. Please. People broke into our house, and Sara's still in there."

"Carl, put your damn gun down. It's Kara and

Caitlyn. You're scaring them. What are you going to do, shoot a baby? And, turn off those damn lights; we don't want them coming here next." Mrs. Teisen pushes her way past Mr. Teisen, and makes her way to us. She takes Caitlyn from me. The first thing she does is remove the blankets around Caitlyn to replace it with one of her own. Carl switches off the lights. "Come on darling. We'll call the sheriff. We'll get you some warm clothes. Get you both warmed up."

And what happens to Sara while we get cozy? I don't know how far away the sheriff is. I don't know if James has even found him yet. "I have to go back."

"Of course, and you'll take Carl with you. But first, you don't even have shoes on, and your clothes are wet. You'll be no use if you have to warm up your feet when you get there." She goes into the front room beside us and lays Caitlyn on the couch. She comes bustling back and right past Mr. Teisen.

"How many were there?" Mr. Teisen asks me. I can see his shadowy figure going into a cabinet. He's rustling around with some things in there. He fills his pockets. I think it might be bullets.

"I don't know. We never saw all of them. There was someone at the bottom of the stairs talking to someone else that made noise in the living room. There's a truck running out front. At least two, three, maybe more." I tell him. I don't want to tell him my theory about Cody and two friends. There could be more, or there might only be two people.

"Mary, call around to all our neighbours and send them over." He switches his attention. "Do you know how to use a gun?"

"No." I never learned beyond shooting squirrels. But dad had always set everything up for me. I just had to take the gun and shoot. I know there is a lot more to it than that. Besides, shooting a person is different than a squirrel with a pea shooter.

He walks over to me. "Take the knife then." He hands me a large hunting knife in a leather holder. I hook the holder onto my pants. I have no idea what I'll do with a knife. It's not like I could actually stab anyone.

Mrs. Teisen comes back. She shoves fabric into my hands; they're socks. "What size of boot are you?"

"Seven." I struggle to keep my balance and put on the socks. She steadies me with her hand on my shoulder.

"You can take one of my boots then. They're eights but they'll work better than nothing." She leaves me briefly, and comes back to set a pair of boots in front of me. Mrs. Teisen runs off down the hallway.

I slip on the socks and boots. When I stand up another lump of fabric is thrown at me. I put the sweater on. It's must be Mr. Teisen's. It's so large.

"Mary, are you calling anyone yet?" Mr. Teisen yells to his wife. I'm not sure where she's run off to.

"Yes, yes. Be careful you two." She yells back at him.

"Lock the door behind us." He yells at her. More quietly he says to me. "Get the knife ready. We're going now. Stay behind me." He leads the way out the door.

I follow after him. The cold air bites, so soon after just partially warming up. Fumbling with the knife holder at first, I am able to get the knife in my hand. Holding it like a kitchen knife.

It's not a far walk to our door. I don't hear any sirens, but that may mean nothing. There are no other movements so I'm not sure how successful Mrs. Teisen is being at getting a hold of anyone. A phone call in the middle of the night is easily ignored.

We walk up to the front door. There still aren't any lights on inside, but every once in a while I can see a light from a flashlight.

With no warning Mr. Teisen bursts through the door. I'm guessing he's going for a surprise factor. Running in after him, all I can think of is getting to Sara. Adrenaline pushes me up the stairs.

There's shouting downstairs. Someone turns on a light. I don't know what I got myself into when there's guns shots. I let out a little bit of a shriek.

Mom's door opens. Cody emerges looking slightly panicked and adjusting his pants. The noticeable bulge in his pants, and sweat on his forehead have me fearing what he's done to Sara. I lurch at him with my knife out. He easily stops me, and pushes me into the wall.

"Where's Caitlyn!?" He yells two inches away from my face.

Like I'm going to tell you. "Fuck you."

That might have been the wrong thing to say. His fist feels like a sledge hammer was brought down unto my face. I get it twice for both punches. Each time his fist hits my face, my head ricochets off the wall.

"WHERE'S CAITLYN!?" He yells at me again.

My eyes are crossed from the daze my head is

in. My body feels like its shut down. Somehow, sometime I lost the knife. I don't think it's my own two legs that are holding me up.

"Safe from you." I close my eyes ready for another beating. It doesn't come. I wait. Something separates us. My body is thrown off balance and onto the ground. I open my eyes, and Sara is in front of me. She has Cody off balance. She pushes him and he falls down the stairs. There are a bunch of thuds, before nothing. I get up to see his body lying at the bottom of the stairs.

Sara turns to me. "You shouldn't have come back." Her voice sounds like she's dead inside.

"She's safe." I try to justify coming back. Walking forward, I brace myself on the railing. Cody doesn't look like he's moving. He's probably dead, but I want to be sure. He doesn't deserve to live.

There's someone rushing into the house with their shot gun drawn. It's drunk Will. He's steady on his feet; though I'm sure he's as drunk as can be. He's got his gun trained on someone. They emerge soon enough with their hands up. Mr. Teisen has his own shot gun on him from behind.

The sheriff finally comes into the house. He raises his revolver to point at the man the other two are pointing at. "Everyone put you guns down! Put them down!" He shouts. Will and Mr. Teisen lower their guns. He immediately goes to the man and puts hand cuffs on him. "Are there any more assailants?"

"I had to shoot one in the kitchen. He shot my arm. I think that's it." Mr. Teisen confesses. The sheriff puts his gun into his holder, and takes the shot gun away from Mr. Teisen.

His two backups come into the house, and go off in different directions to search the house. James runs in with another medic and assesses Cody quickly. He doesn't take long to say, "He's out cold." His partner goes into the back of the house, while James comes upstairs.

I must look really bad because he goes to me first. "Sara, are you alright?" He looks over to Sara. I'm not sure who he thinks he's talking to.

"Ya I'm fine, but he punched Kara really hard a few times. Kara where's Caitlyn?" She seems about ready to leap down the stairs to find her.

"She's with Mrs. Teisen." James draws my attention back to him. He's done looking at my face. I see Sara go around us to get downstairs, and probably to get Caitlyn.

"Kara, I need you to follow my finger." I do as he says. He does a couple of things to me. "We should get you in for a scan. To make sure there isn't any internal bleeding. I think you've just got a concussion, but I want to make sure that's it."

"Ya no problem." My eyes flick to movement going out the door. Cody's body is gone.

Goosebumps creep all over my body. He wasn't passed out.

I bolt down the stairs and out the door.

"Kara!" He yells after me. "Shit!"

Two people are fighting in between the two properties.

A gun shot bangs as I approach. I freeze.

One body crumples to the snow; Sara crumples to the snow.

The larger figure turns around and sways. Cody grabs at his chest. As he falls I see the glint from the knife that was just inside his chest.

I run to my sister. Her own chest is bleeding. Blood runs from her mouth. "Sara."

Steve kneels down on the other side of Sara. He opens his medic bag and grabs medical implements to help her.

"Kare, take Caitlyn and leave." She rasps. Tears rolls down her cheeks. Her chest stops moving.

My heart stops beating for a moment. It jumpstarts when a set of hands pull me up and out of the way as Steve starts to work on Sara.

I want to tell him it's useless, that she's dead, but a part of me holds hope that he can revive her.

Mr. Teisen is there when I look over my shoulder. He pushes and guides me into his house where his wife greets the both of us with a big hug.

I let her guide me to the table where Caitlyn is sitting and drinking something out of a mug.

Mrs. Teisen busies herself getting a couple drinks made, and orders Mr. Teisen to get a blanket out of the linen closet.

A knock on the door startles me from my staring at the little girl across the table from me.

Mrs. Teisen sets down a mug filled with hot chocolate in front of me before she goes to the front door.

The sheriff comes out from behind the wall. I look at his solemn expression. I know what is coming, but nothing prepares me for it.

My world stops as he tells me, "I'm sorry Kara. There was nothing we could do to save her."

Chapter 10

"I swear Halloween ends and the very next day they're putting up Christmas decorations." I complain to the tiny girl in the shopping cart. Not that she'll respond to me, but I've taken on the habit of talking to her as if she's got a full conversational capacity.

Two days into November and all trace of Halloween has been eliminated.

I take us to the baby section. This time I grab two boxes of diapers. They do not make these diaper boxes big enough. On a whim I pick up Pull-ups. Maybe this will help with her potty training. This kid is so stubborn. Just when I think she's got it and we go a full day on the potty, then the next she has accidents the whole day. Or we have her good over the weekend, but as soon as Monday comes and she's back at daycare, she loses all progress.

This kid will never lose the diapers. Maybe not never, but not anytime soon.

I know it'll happen eventually, but I want it to happen now. I'd even take her half potty trained, and just do her business in a toilet during the day.

She's growing out of her clothes, so I stop in the clothing section for her. There is one wall worth that have her size, but I don't find anything cute enough.

Time to find another store with cheap enough clothes for her. I've spent more on her clothes in the last month than I have on my clothes in the last year, and that's saying something with the expensive office clothes I have to buy.

Kids are expensive. Her day care expenses alone are as much as my rent. I feel especially broke at the beginning of the month now.

I shake my head loose from the thoughts. She's lucky she's cute, and I love her.

We go to the check out, waiting three people in line to get to the cashier.

She checks us out with a smile, and fawning over Caitlyn.

When we finally leave, I usher her into her car seat, and pile our supplies in the trunk. I leave the cart there beside my car, because I forgot to put it away before putting Caitlyn into the car seat. I'm paranoid that someone would notice she's in there alone and call the cops on me, or break the window to free her, or even try to kidnap her.

Parenthood has made me paranoid.

The short trip back to the apartment is enough to let her fall asleep. I sigh. This will mean the diapers will have to stay in the trunk until she wakes up. Either that or she'll be left alone in the apartment or the car seat, which I can't do.

Paranoia strikes once again. I wouldn't want someone to find out. I always imagine child protection services getting called, and Caitlyn being removed from my custody.

Cody's parents have already pushed to request they be made her guardians rather than me. My saving grace was no will, and Steve vouching that Sara had requested me in her last breath.

I don't want to give anyone any reason why someone else should raise Caitlyn. She's the last bit I have of my sister, and I won't give her up because of something stupid.

I let her loose of her restraint and pick her out. She wakes momentarily, but falls quickly back into slumber as I rest her on my shoulder. I grab her bag and lock the car.

The long trek up to my door is strenuous with the added weight of the toddler and the equally heavy diaper bag.

It's a relief when I get into my apartment and can set down the bag. Leaving my shoes at the door, I go down to Caitlyn's room. If I manage to get her down into her bed without waking her, it will be a miracle; about a fifty/fifty chance she'll wake up.

Leaning against the bed, I start a slow lowering of her and my torso into the drawn sheets. When my hands hit the mattress I pull up my torso. She's still asleep. Pushing my hands deeper into the mattress I manage to pull them free without waking her.

Success.

Covering her with the blanket is no problem. I blow her a kiss and walk out of the room; closing the door behind me.

A picture of her mom greets me across from her room. It is a picture of Sara and Caitlyn I had snapped while there. Nothing too special about the living room backdrop but it was taken without their knowing.

No fake smiles from a self-conscious mother. No goofy smiles from the little girl told to say cheese.

Real smiles from a daughter cuddling her mom as they contently watch a movie.

It's my favourite picture of them, and one of the only pictures of the two of them which wasn't taken as a selfie.

I miss her. My nose tingles, and my eyes start

to fill with tears.

Averting my eyes and taking a deep breath in, I stop them from falling. I don't have time to spend all of Caitlyn's nap crying.

There are toys to put away, messes to clean, floors to mop, supper to make, and laundry to be done.

Life to continually move forward for the sake of all involved.

www.ingramcontent.com/pod-product-compliance
Lightning Source LLC
Chambersburg PA
CBHW020621120726
47905CB00003B/884